His shirt was open to the third button, his silk tie hanging loose around his neck in the classic, clichéd image from every red-blooded woman's slickest fantasy. But that was where the dream ended, because Kit's face was like chiselled marble and his hooded eyes were as cold as ice.

And in that second, in a rush of horror and pain, his expression—completely deadpan apart from the slight curl of his lip as he looked at her across the space that separated them—said it all.

'You unutterable bastard,' she breathed.

She didn't wait for a response. Somehow she made her trembling legs carry her out of the wine cellar and along the corridor, while her horrified mind struggled to take in the enormity of what had just happened. She had proved Kit Fitzroy right. She had played straight into his hands and revealed herself as the faithless, worthless gold-digger he'd taken her for all along.

Award-winning author

India Grey

presents
The Fitzroy Legacy

Wedlocked to the aristocratic Fitzroy family
—where shocking secrets lead to scandalous seduction

The epic romance of Kit and Sophie begins with...
CRAVING THE FORBIDDEN
On sale October 2011

And concludes with
IN BED WITH A STRANGER
On sale December 2011

Can you wait to find out what happens...?

CRAVING THE FORBIDDEN

BY
INDIA GREY

First published in Great Britain 2011
by Mills & Boon, an imprint of Harlequin (UK) Limited,
Eton House, 18-24 Paradise Road, Richmond, Surrey TW9 1SR

© India Grey 2011

ISBN: 978 0 263 22094 0

CRAVING THE
FORBIDDEN

For my blog regulars

With thanks for listening, sharing and making me smile.

CHAPTER ONE

'LADIES and gentlemen, welcome aboard the 16.22 East Coast Mainline service from King's Cross to Edinburgh. This train will be calling at Peterborough, Stevenage…'

Heart hammering against her ribs from the mad, last-minute dash down the platform carrying a bag that was about to burst at the seams, Sophie Greenham leaned against the wall of the train and let out a long exhalation of relief.

She had made it.

Of course, the relief was maybe a little misplaced given that she'd come straight from the casting session for a vampire film and was still wearing a black satin corset dress that barely covered her bottom and high-heeled black boots that were rather more vamp than vampire. But the main thing was she had caught the train and wouldn't let Jasper down. She'd just have to keep her coat on to avoid getting arrested for indecent exposure.

Not that she'd want to take it off anyway, she thought grimly, wrapping it more tightly around her as the train gave a little lurch and began to move. For weeks now the snow had kept falling from a pewter-grey sky and the news headlines had been dominated by The Big Freeze. Paris had been just as bad, although there the snow *looked* cleaner, but when Sophie had left her little rented apartment two days ago there had been a thick layer of ice on the inside of the windows.

She seemed to have been cold for an awfully long time.

It was getting dark already. The plate-glass windows of the office blocks backing onto the railway line spilled light out onto the grimy snow. The train swayed beneath her, changing tracks and catching her off guard so that she tottered on the stupid high-heeled boots and almost fell into an alarmed-looking student on his way back from the buffet car. She really should go and find a loo to change into something more respectable, but now she'd finally stopped rushing she was overwhelmed with tiredness. Picking up her bag, she hoisted it awkwardly into the nearest carriage.

Her heart sank. It was instantly obvious that every seat was taken, and the aisle was cluttered with shopping bags and briefcases and heavy winter coats stuffed under seats. Muttering apologies as she staggered along, trying not to knock cardboard cartons of coffee out of the hands of commuters with her bag, she made her way into the next carriage.

It was just as bad as the last one. The feeling of triumph she'd had when she'd made it onto the train in time ebbed slowly away as she moved from one carriage to the next, apologising as she went, until finally she came to one that was far less crowded.

Sophie's aching shoulders dropped in relief. And tensed again as she took in the strip of plush carpet, the tiny lights on the tables, the superior upholstery with the little covers over the headrests saying 'First Class'.

Pants.

It was occupied almost entirely by businessmen who didn't bother to look up from their laptops and newspapers as she passed. Until her mobile rang. Her ringtone—'Je Ne Regrette Rien'—had seemed wittily ironic in Paris, but in the hushed carriage it lost some of its charm. Holding the handles of her bag together in one hand while she scrabbled in the pocket of her coat with the other and tried to stop it falling open to reveal the wardrobe horror beneath, she was aware of heads turning, eyes looking up at her over the tops of glasses and from behind broadsheets. In desperation she hitched her bag onto the nearest table and pulled the phone from her pocket just in time to see Jean-Claude's name on the screen.

Pants again.

A couple of months ago she would have had a very different reaction, she thought, hastily pressing the button to reject the call. But then a couple of months ago her image of Jean-Claude as a free-spirited Parisian artist had been intact. He'd seemed so aloof when she'd first seen him, delivering paintings to the set of the film she was working on. Aloof and glamorous. Not someone you could ever imagine being suffocating or possessive or...

Nope. She wasn't going to think about the disaster that had been her latest romantic adventure.

She sat down in the nearest seat, suddenly too tired to go any further. You couldn't keep moving for ever, she told herself with a stab of bleak humour. In the seat opposite there was yet another businessman, hidden behind a large newspaper that he'd thoughtfully folded so that the horoscopes were facing her.

Actually, he wasn't *entirely* hidden; she could see his hands, holding the newspaper—tanned, long-fingered, strong-looking. Not the hands of a businessman, she thought abstractly, tearing her gaze away and looking for Libra. 'Be prepared to work hard to make a good impression,' she read. 'The full moon on the 20th is a perfect opportunity to let others see you for who you really are.'

Hell. It was the twentieth today. And while she was prepared to put on an Oscar-worthy performance to impress Jasper's family, the last thing she wanted was for them to see her for who she really was.

At that moment Edith Piaf burst into song again. She

groaned—why couldn't Jean-Claude take a hint? Quickly she went to shut Edith up and turn her phone off but at that moment the train swayed again and her finger accidentally hit the 'answer' button instead. A second later Jean-Claude's Merlot-marinated voice was clearly audible, to her and about fifteen businessmen.

'Sophie? Sophie, where are you—?'

She thought quickly, cutting him off before he had a chance to get any further. 'Hello, you haf reached the voicemail service for Madame Sofia, astrologist and reader of cards,' she purred, shaking her hair back and narrowing her eyes at her own reflection in the darkening glass of the window. 'Eef you leaf your name, number and zodiac sign, I get back to you with information on what the fates haf in store for you—'

She stopped abruptly, losing her thread, a kick of electricity jolting through her as she realised she was staring straight into the reflected eyes of the man sitting opposite.

Or rather that, from behind the newspaper, *he* was staring straight into *her* eyes. His head was lowered, his face ghostly in the glass, but his dark eyes seemed to look straight into her.

For a second she was helpless to do anything but look back. Against the stark white of his shirt his skin was tanned, which seemed somehow at odds with his stern, ascetic face. It was the face of a medieval knight in a Pre-Raphaelite painting— beautiful, bloodless, remote.

In other words, absolutely not her type.

'Sophie—is zat you? I can 'ardly 'ear you. Are you on Eurostar? Tell me what time you get in and I meet you at Gare du Nord.'

Oops, she'd forgotten all about Jean-Claude. Gathering herself, she managed to drag her gaze away from the reflection in the window and her attention back to the problem quite literally in hand. She'd better just come clean, or he'd keep ringing for the whole weekend she was staying with Jasper's family and rather ruin her portrayal of the sweet, starry-eyed girlfriend.

'I'm not on the Eurostar, no,' she said carefully. 'I'm not coming back tonight.'

'*Alors*, when?' he demanded. 'The painting—I need you here. I need to see your skin—to feel it, to capture contrast with lily petals.'

'Nude with Lilies' was the vision Jean-Claude claimed had come to him the moment he'd first noticed her in a bar in the Marais, near where they'd been filming. Jasper had been over that weekend and thought it was hilarious. Sophie, hugely flattered to be singled out and by Jean-Claude's extravagant compliments about her 'skin like lily petals' and 'hair like flames', had thought being painted would be a highly erotic experience.

The reality had turned out to be both extremely cold and mind-numbingly boring. Although, if Jean-Claude's gaze had aroused a similar reaction to that provoked by the eyes of the man in the glass, it would have been a very different story...

'Oh, dear. Maybe you could just paint in a few more lilies to cover up the skin?' She bit back a breathless giggle and went on kindly, 'Look, I don't know when I'll be back, but what we had wasn't meant to be for ever, was it? Really, it was just sex—'

Rather fittingly, at that point the train whooshed into a tunnel and the signal was lost. Against the blackness beyond the window the reflected interior of the carriage was bright, and for the briefest moment Sophie caught the eye of the man opposite and knew he'd been looking at her again. The grey remains of the daylight made the reflection fade before she had time to read the expression on his face, but she was left in no doubt that it had been disapproving.

And in that second she was eight years old again, holding her mother's hand and aware that people were staring at them, judging them. The old humiliation flared inside her as she heard her mother's voice inside her head, strident with indignation. *Just ignore them, Summer. We have as much right to be here as anyone else...*

'Sophie?'

'Yes,' she said, suddenly subdued. 'Sorry, Jean-Claude. I can't talk about this now. I'm on the train and the signal isn't very good.'

'*D'accord.* I call you later.'

'No! You can't call me *at all* this weekend. I-I'm...working, and you know I can't take my phone on set. Look, I'll call you when I get back to London on Monday. We can talk properly then.'

That was a stupid thing to say, she thought wearily as she turned her phone off. There was nothing to talk *about*. What she and Jean-Claude had shared had been fun, that was all. Fun. A romantic adventure in wintry Paris. Now it had reached its natural conclusion and it was time to move on.

Again.

Shoving her phone back into her pocket, she turned towards the window. Outside it was snowing again and, passing through some anonymous town, Sophie could see the flakes swirling fatly in the streetlamps and obliterating the footprints on the pavements, and rows of neat houses, their curtains shut against the winter evening. She imagined the people behind them; families slumped together in front of the TV, arguing cosily over the remote control, couples cuddled up on the sofa sharing a Friday evening bottle of wine, united against the cold world outside.

A blanket of depression settled on her at these mental images of comfortable domesticity. It was a bit of a sore point at the moment. Returning from Paris she'd discovered that, in her absence, her flatmate's boyfriend had moved in and the flat had been turned into the headquarters of the Blissful Couples Society. The atmosphere of companionable sluttishness in which she and Jess had existed, cluttering up the place with make-up and laundry and trashy magazines, had vanished. The flat was immaculate, and there were new cushions on the sofa and candles on the kitchen table.

Jasper's SOS phone call, summoning her up to his family home in Northumberland to play the part of his girlfriend for the weekend, had come as a huge relief. But this was the way it was going to be, she thought sadly as the town was left behind and the train plunged onwards into darkness again. Everyone pairing up, until she was the only single person left, the only one who actively didn't want a relationship or commitment. Even Jasper was showing worrying signs of swapping late nights and dancing for cosy evenings in as things got serious with Sergio.

But why have serious when you could have *fun*?

Getting abruptly to her feet, she picked up her bag and hoisted it onto the luggage rack above her head. It wasn't easy, and she was aware as she pushed and shoved that not only was the hateful dress riding up, but her coat had also fallen open, no doubt giving the man in the seat opposite an eyeful of straining black corset and an indecent amount of thigh. Prickling all over with embarrassment, she glanced at his reflection in the window.

He wasn't looking at her at all. His head was tipped back against the seat, his face completely blank and remote as he focused on the newspaper. Somehow his indifference felt even more hurtful than his disapproving scrutiny earlier. Pulling her coat closed, she sat down again, but as she did so her knee grazed his thigh beneath the table.

She froze, and a shower of glowing sparks shimmered through her.

'Sorry,' she muttered, yanking her legs away from his and tucking them underneath her on the seat.

Slowly the newspaper was lowered, and she found herself looking at him directly for the first time. The impact of meeting his eyes in glassy reflection had been powerful enough, but looking directly into them was like touching a live wire. They weren't brown, as she'd thought, but the grey of cold Northern seas, heavy-lidded, fringed with thick, dark lashes, compelling enough to distract her for a moment from the rest of his face.

Until he smiled.

A faint ghost of a smile that utterly failed to melt the ice in his eyes, but did draw her attention down to his mouth…

'No problem. As this is First Class you'd think there'd be enough legroom, wouldn't you?'

His voice was low and husky, and so sexy that her spirits should have leapt at the prospect of spending the next four hours in close confinement with him. However, the slightly scornful emphasis he placed on the words 'first' and 'class' and the way he was looking at her as if she were a caterpillar on the chef's salad in some swanky restaurant cancelled out his physical attractiveness.

She had issues with people who looked at her like that.

'Absolutely,' she agreed, with that upper-class self-assurance that gave the people who genuinely possessed it automatic admittance to anywhere. 'Shocking, really.' And then with what she hoped was utter insouciance she turned up the big collar of her shabby military-style coat, settled herself more comfortably in her seat and closed her eyes.

Kit Fitzroy put down the newspaper.

Usually when he was on leave he avoided reading reports about the situation he'd left behind; somehow the heat and the sand and the desperation never quite came across in columns of sterile black and white. He'd bought the newspaper to catch up on normal things like rugby scores and racing news, but had ended up reading all of it in an attempt to obliterate the image of the girl sitting opposite him, which seemed to have branded itself onto his retinas.

It hadn't worked. Even the laughably inaccurate report of counter-terrorist operations in the Middle East hadn't stopped him being aware of her.

It was hardly surprising, he thought acidly. He'd spent the last four months marooned in the desert with a company made up entirely of men, and he was still human enough to respond to a girl wearing stiletto boots and the briefest bondage dress beneath a fake army coat. Especially one with a husky night-club singer's voice who actually seemed to be complaining to the lovesick fool on the other end of the phone that all she'd wanted was casual sex.

After the terrible sombreness of the ceremony he'd just attended her appearance was like a swift shot of something extremely potent.

He suppressed a rueful smile.

Potent, if not particularly sophisticated.

He let his gaze move back to her. She had fallen asleep as quickly and neatly as a cat, her legs tucked up beneath her, a slight smile on her raspberry-pink lips, as if she was dreaming of something amusing. She had a sweep of black eyeliner on her upper lids, flicking up at the outside edges, which must be what gave her eyes their catlike impression.

He frowned. No—it wasn't just that. It was their striking green too. He could picture their exact shade—the clear, cool green of new leaves—even now, when she was fast asleep.

If she really was asleep. When it came to deception Kit Fitzroy's radar was pretty accurate, and this girl had set it off from the moment she'd appeared. But there was something about her now that convinced him that she wasn't faking this.

It wasn't just how still she was, but that the energy that had crackled around her before had vanished. It was like a light going out. Like the sun going in, leaving shadows and a sudden chill.

Sleep—the reward of the innocent. Given the shamelessness with which she'd just lied to her boyfriend it didn't seem fair, especially when it eluded him so cruelly. But it had wrapped her in a cloak of complete serenity, so that just looking at her, just watching the lock of bright coppery hair that had fallen across her face stir with each soft, steady breath made him aware of the ache of exhaustion in his own shoulders.

'Tickets, please.'

The torpor that lay over the warm carriage was disturbed by the arrival of the guard. There was a ripple of activity as people roused themselves to open briefcases and fumble in suit pockets. On the opposite side of the table the girl's sooty lashes didn't even flutter.

She was older than he'd first thought, Kit saw now, older than the ridiculous teenage get-up would suggest—in her mid-twenties perhaps? Even so, there was something curiously childlike about her. If you ignored the creamy swell of her cleavage against the laced bodice of her dress, anyway.

And he was doing his best to ignore it.

The guard reached them, his bland expression changing to one of deep discomfort when he looked down and saw her. His tongue flicked nervously across his lips and he raised his hand, shifting from foot to foot as he reached uneasily down to wake her.

'Don't.'

The guard looked round, surprised. He wasn't the only one, Kit thought. Where had that come from? He smiled blandly.

'It's OK. She's with me.'

'Sorry, sir. I didn't realise. Do you have your tickets?'

'No.' Kit flipped open his wallet. 'I—*we*—had been planning to travel north by plane.'

'Ah, I see, sir. The weather has caused quite a disruption to flights, I understand. That's why the train is so busy this evening. Is it a single or a return you want?'

'Return.' Hopefully the airports would be open again by Sunday, but he wasn't taking any chances. The thought of being stuck indefinitely at Alnburgh with his family in residence was unbearable.

'Two returns—to Edinburgh?'

Kit nodded absently and as the guard busied himself with printing out the tickets he looked back at the sleeping girl again. He was damned certain she didn't have a first-class ticket and that, in spite of the almost-convincing posh-girl accent, she wouldn't be buying one if she was challenged. So why had he not just let the guard wake her up and move her on? It would have made the rest of the journey better for him. More legroom. More peace of mind.

Kit Fitzroy had an inherent belief in his duty to look out for people who didn't have the same privileges that he had. It was what had got him through officer training and what kept him going when he was dropping with exhaustion on patrol, or when he was walking along a deserted road to an unexploded bomb. It didn't usually compel him to buy first-class tickets for strangers on the train. And anyway, this girl looked as if she was more than capable of looking after herself.

But with her outrageous clothes and her fiery hair and her slight air of mischief she had brightened up his journey. She'd jolted him out of the pall of gloom that hung over him after the service he'd just attended, as well as providing a distraction from thinking about the grim weekend ahead.

That had to be worth the price of a first-class ticket from London to Edinburgh. Even without the glimpse of cleavage and the brush of her leg against his, which had reminded him that, while several of the men he'd served with weren't so lucky, he at least was still alive...

That was just a bonus.

CHAPTER TWO

SOPHIE came to with a start, and a horrible sense that something was wrong.

She sat up, blinking beneath the bright lights as she tried to get her bearings. The seat opposite was empty. The man with the silver eyes must have got off while she was sleeping, and she was just asking herself why on earth she should feel disappointed about that when she saw him.

He was standing up, his back towards her as he lifted an expensive-looking leather bag down from the luggage rack, giving her an excellent view of his extremely broad shoulders and narrow hips encased in beautifully tailored black trousers.

Mmm… *That* was why, she thought drowsily. Because physical perfection like that wasn't something you came across every day. And although it might come in a package with industrial-strength arrogance, it certainly was nice to look at.

'I'm sorry—could you tell me where we are, please?'

Damn—she'd forgotten about the posh accent, and after being asleep for so long she sounded more like a barmaid with a sixty-a-day habit than a wholesome society girl. Not that it really mattered now, since she'd never see him again.

He shrugged on the kind of expensive reefer jacket men

wore in moody black and white adverts in glossy magazines. 'Alnburgh.'

The word delivered a jolt of shock to Sophie's sleepy brain. With an abrupt curse she leapt to her feet, groping frantically for her things, but at that moment the train juddered to an abrupt halt. She lost her balance, falling straight into his arms.

At least that was how it would have happened in any one of the romantic films she'd ever worked on. In reality she didn't so much fall into his waiting, welcoming arms as against the unyielding, rock-hard wall of his chest. He caught hold of her in the second before she ricocheted off him, one arm circling her waist like a band of steel. Rushing to steady herself, Sophie automatically put the flat of her hand against his chest.

Sexual recognition leapt into life inside her, like an alarm going off in her pelvis. He might look lean, but there was no mistaking the hard, sculpted muscle beneath the Savile Row shirt.

Wide-eyed with shock, she looked up at him, opening her mouth in an attempt to form some sort of apology. But somehow there were blank spaces in her head where the words should be and the only coherent thought in her head was how astonishing his eyes were, close up; the silvery luminescence of the irises ringed with a darker grey...

'I have to get off—now,' she croaked.

It wasn't exactly a line from the romantic epics. He let her go abruptly, turning his head away.

'It's OK. We're not in the station yet.'

As he spoke the train began to move forwards with another jolt that threatened to unbalance her again. As if she weren't unbalanced enough already, she thought shakily, trying to pull down her bulging bag from where it was wedged in the luggage rack. Glancing anxiously out of the window, she saw the lights of cars waiting at a level crossing slide past the window, a little square signal box, cosily lit inside, with a sign saying 'Alnburgh' half covered in snow. She gave another futile tug and heard an impatient sound from behind her.

'Here, let me.'

In one lithe movement he leaned over her and grasped the handle of her bag.

'No, wait—the zip—' Sophie yelped, but it was too late. There was a ripping sound as the cheap zip, already under too much pressure from the sheer volume of stuff bundled up inside, gave way and Sophie watched in frozen horror as a tangle of dresses and tights and shoes tumbled out.

And underwear, of course.

It was terrible. Awful. Like the moment in a nightmare just before you wake up. But it was also pretty funny. Clamping a hand over her open mouth, Sophie couldn't stop a bubble of hysterical laughter escaping her.

'You might want to take that back to the shop,' the man remarked sardonically, reaching up to unhook an emerald-green satin balcony bra that had got stuck on the edge of the luggage rack. 'I believe Gucci luggage carries a lifetime guarantee?'

Sophie dropped to her knees to retrieve the rest of her things. Possibly it did, but cheap designer fakes certainly didn't, as he no doubt knew very well. Getting up again, she couldn't help but be aware of the length of his legs, and had to stop herself from reaching out and grabbing hold of them to steady herself as the train finally came to a shuddering halt in the station.

'Thanks for your help,' she said with as much haughtiness as she could muster when her arms were full of knickers and tights. 'Please, don't let me hold you up any more.'

'I wouldn't, except you're blocking the way to the door.'

Sophie felt her face turn fiery. Pressing herself as hard as she could against the table, she tried to make enough space for him to pass. But he didn't. Instead he took hold of the broken bag and lifted it easily, raising one sardonic eyebrow.

'After you—if you've got everything?'

Alnburgh station consisted of a single Victorian building that had once been rather beautiful but which now had its boarded up windows covered with posters advertising family days out at the seaside. It was snowing again as she stepped off the train, and the air felt as if it had swept straight in from Siberia. Oh, dear, she really should have got changed. Not only was her current ensemble hideously unsuitable for meeting Jasper's family, it was also likely to lead to hypothermia.

'There.'

Sophie had no choice but to turn and face him. Pulling her collar up around her neck, she aimed for a sort of Julie-Christie-in-Doctor-Zhivago look—determination mixed with dignity.

'You'll be OK from here?'

'Y-yes. Thank you.' Standing there with the snow settling on his shoulders and in his dark hair he looked more brooding and sexy than Omar Shariff had ever done in the film. 'And thank you for...'

Jeepers, what was the matter with her? Julie Christie would never have let her lines dry up like that.

'For what?'

'Oh, you know, carrying my bag, picking up my...things.'

'My pleasure.'

His eyes met hers and for a second their gazes held. In spite of the cold stinging her cheeks, Sophie felt a tide of heat rise up inside her.

And then the moment was over and he was turning away, his feet crunching on the gritted paving stones, sliding his hands into the pockets of his coat just as the guard blew the whistle for the train to move out of the station again.

That was what reminded her, like a bolt of lightning in her brain. Clamping her hand to her mouth, she felt horror tingle down her spine at the realisation that she hadn't bought a ticket. Letting out a yelp of horror, followed by the kind of word Julie Christie would never use, Sophie dashed forwards towards the guard, whose head was sticking out of the window of his van.

'No—wait. Please! I didn't—'

But it was too late. The train was gathering pace and her voice was lost beneath the rumble of the engine and the squealing of the metal wheels on the track. As she watched the lights of the train melt back into the winter darkness Sophie's heart was beating hard, anguish knotting inside her at what she'd inadvertently done.

Stolen something. That was what it amounted to, didn't it? Travelling on the train without buying a ticket was, in effect, committing a criminal act, as well as a dishonest one.

An act of theft.

And that was one thing she would never, *ever* do.

The clatter of the train died in the distance and Sophie was aware of the silence folding all around her. Slowly she turned to walk back to pick up her forlorn-looking bag.

'Is there a problem?'

Her stomach flipped, and then sank like a stone. Great. Captain Disapproval must have heard her shout and come back, thinking she was talking to him. The station light cast dark shadows beneath his cheekbones and made him look more remote than ever. Which was quite something.

'No, no, not at all,' she said stiffly. 'Although before you go perhaps you could tell me where I could find a taxi.'

Kit couldn't quite stop himself from letting out a bark of laughter. It wasn't kind, but the idea of a taxi waiting at Alnburgh station was amusingly preposterous.

'You're not in London now.' He glanced down the platform

to where the Bentley waited, Jensen sitting impassively behind the wheel. For some reason he felt responsible—touched almost—by this girl in her outrageous clothing with the snowflakes catching in her bright hair. 'Look, you'd better come with me.'

Her chin shot up half an inch. Her eyes flashed in the station light—the dark green of the stained glass in the Fitzroy family chapel, with the light shining through it.

'No, thanks,' she said with brittle courtesy. 'I think I'd rather walk.'

That really *was* funny. 'In those boots?'

'Yes,' she said haughtily, setting off quickly, if a little unsteadily, along the icy platform. She looked around, pulling her long army overcoat more tightly across her body.

Catching up with her, Kit arched an eyebrow. 'Don't tell me,' he drawled. 'You're going to join your regiment.'

'No,' she snapped. 'I'm going to stay with my boyfriend, who lives at Alnburgh Castle. So if you could just point me in the right direction…'

Kit stopped. The laughter of a moment ago evaporated in the arctic air, like the plumes of their breaths. In the distance a sheep bleated mournfully.

'And what is the name of your…*boyfriend*?'

Something in the tone of his voice made her stop too, the metallic echo of her stiletto heels fading into silence. When she turned to face him her eyes were wide and black-centred.

'Jasper.' Her voice was shaky but defiant. 'Jasper Fitzroy, although I don't know what it has to do with you.'

Kit smiled again, but this time it had nothing to do with amusement.

'Well, since Jasper Fitzroy is my brother, I'd say quite a lot,' he said with sinister softness. 'You'd better get in the car.'

CHAPTER THREE

INSIDE the chauffeur-driven Bentley Sophie blew her cheeks out in a long, silent whistle.

What was it that horoscope said?

The car was very warm and very comfortable, but no amount of climate control and expensive upholstery could quite thaw the glacial atmosphere. Apart from a respectfully murmured 'Good evening, Miss,' the chauffeur kept his attention very firmly focused on the road. Sophie didn't blame him. You could cut the tension in the back of the car with a knife.

Sophie sat very upright, leaving as much seat as possible between her fishnetted thigh and his long, hard flannel-covered one. She didn't dare look at Jasper's brother, but was aware of him staring, tense-jawed, out of the window. The village of Alnburgh looked like a scene from a Christmas card as they drove up the main street, past a row of stone houses with low, gabled roofs covered in a crisp meringue-topping of snow, but he didn't look very pleased to be home.

Her mind raced as crazily as the white flakes swirling past the car window, the snatches of information Jasper had imparted about his brother over the years whirling through it. Kit Fitzroy was in the army, she knew that much, and he served abroad a lot, which would account for the unseasonal tan. Oh, and Jasper had once described him as having a 'complete emotion-bypass'. She recalled the closed expression Jasper's face wore on the rare occasions he mentioned him, the bitter edge his habitual mocking sarcasm took on when he said the words 'my brother'.

She was beginning to understand why. She had only known him for a little over three hours—and most of that time she'd been asleep—but it was enough to find it impossible to believe that this man could be related to Jasper. Sweet, warm, funny Jasper, who was her best friend in the world and the closest thing she had to family.

But the man beside her was his *real* flesh and blood, so surely that meant he couldn't be all bad? It also meant that she should make some kind of effort to get on with him, for Jasper's sake. And her own, since she had to get through an entire weekend in his company.

'So, you must be Kit, then?' she offered. 'I'm Sophie. Sophie Greenham.' She laughed—a habit she had when she was nervous. 'Bizarre, isn't it? Whoever would have guessed we were going to the same place?'

Kit Fitzroy didn't bother to look at her. 'Not you, obviously. Have you known my brother long?'

OK. So she was wrong. He was every bit as bad as she'd first thought. Thinking of the horoscope, she bit back the urge to snap, *Yes, as a matter of fact. I've known your brother for the last seven years, as you would have been very well aware if you took the slightest interest in him*, and kept her voice saccharine sweet as she recited the story she and Jasper had hastily come up with last night on the phone when he'd asked her to do this.

'Just since last summer. We met on a film.'

The last bit at least was true. Jasper was an assistant director and they had met on a dismal film about the Black Death that mercifully had never seen the light of day. Sophie had spent hours in make-up having sores applied to her face and had had one line to say, but had caught Jasper's eye just as she'd been about to deliver it and noticed that he was shaking with laughter. It had set her off too, and made the next four hours and twenty-two takes extremely challenging, but it had also sealed their friendship, and set its tone. It had been the two of them, united and giggling against the world, ever since.

He turned his head slightly. 'You're an actress?'

'Yes.'

Damn, why did that come out sounding so defensive? Possibly because he said the word 'actress' in the same faintly disdainful tone as other people might say 'lap dancer' or 'shoplifter'. What would he make of the fact that even 'actress' was stretching it for the bit parts she did in films and TV series? Clamping her teeth together, she looked away—and gasped.

Up ahead, lit up in the darkness, cloaked in swirling white like a fairy castle in a child's snow globe, was Alnburgh Castle.

She'd seen pictures, obviously. But nothing had prepared her for the scale of the place, or the impact it made on the surrounding landscape. It stood on top of the cliffs, its grey stone walls seeming to rise directly out of them. This was a side of Jasper's life she knew next to nothing about, and Sophie felt her mouth fall open as she stared in amazement.

'Bloody hell,' she breathed.

It was the first genuine reaction he'd seen her display, Kit thought sardonically, watching her. And it spoke volumes.

Sympathy wasn't an emotion he was used to experiencing in relation to Jasper, but at that moment he certainly felt something like it now. His brother must be pretty keen on this girl to invite her up here for Ralph Fitzroy's seventieth birthday party, but from what Kit had seen on the train it was obvious the feeling wasn't remotely mutual.

No prizes for guessing what the attraction was for Sophie Greenham.

'Impressive, isn't it?' he remarked acidly.

In the dimly lit interior of the car her eyes gleamed darkly like moonlit pools as she turned to face him. Her voice was breathless, so that she sounded almost intimidated.

'It's incredible. I had no idea...'

'What, that your boyfriend just happened to be the son of the Earl of Hawksworth?' Kit murmured sardonically. 'Of course. You were probably too busy discussing your mutual love of art-house cinema to get round to such mundane subjects as family background.'

'Don't be ridiculous,' she snapped. 'Of course I knew about Jasper's background—*and* his family.'

She said that last bit with a kind of defiant venom that was clearly meant to let him know that Jasper hadn't given him a good press. He wondered if she thought for a moment that he'd care. It was hardly a well-kept secret that there was no love lost between him and his brother—the spoiled, pampered golden boy. Ralph's second and favourite son.

The noise of the Bentley's engine echoed off the walls of the clock tower as they passed through the arch beneath it. The headlights illuminated the stone walls, dripping with damp, the iron-studded door that led down to the former dungeon that now housed Ralph's wine cellar. Kit felt the invisible iron-hard bands of tension around his chest and his forehead tighten a couple of notches.

It was funny, he spent much of his time in the most dangerous conflict zones on the globe, but in none of them did he ever feel a fraction as isolated or exposed as he did here. When he was working he had his team behind him. Men he could trust.

Trust wasn't something he'd ever associated with home

life at Alnburgh, where people told lies and kept secrets and made promises they didn't keep.

He glanced across at the woman sitting beside him, and felt his lip curl. Jasper's new girlfriend was going to fit in very well.

Sophie didn't wait until the chauffeur came round to open the door for her. The moment the car came to a standstill she reached for the handle and threw the door open, desperate to be out of the confined space with Kit Fitzroy.

A gust of salt-scented, ice-edged wind cleared her head but nearly knocked her sideways, whipping her hair across her face. Impatiently she brushed it away again. Alnburgh Castle loomed ahead of her. And above her and around her too, she thought weakly, turning to look at the fortress-thick walls that stretched into the darkness all around her, rising into huge, imposing buildings and jagged towers.

There was nothing remotely welcoming or inviting about it. Everything about the place was designed to scare people off and keep them out.

Sophie could see that Jasper's brother would be right at home here.

'Thanks, Jensen. I can manage the bags from here.'

'If you're sure, sir...'

Sophie turned in time to see Kit take her bag from the open boot of the Bentley and turn to walk in the direction of the castle's vast, imposing doorway. One strap of the green satin bra he had picked up on the train was hanging out of the top of it.

Hastily she hurried after him, her high heels ringing off the frozen flagstones and echoing around the walls of the castle courtyard.

'Please,' Sophie persisted, not wanting him to put himself

out on her account any more than he had—so unwillingly—done already. 'I'd rather take it myself.'

He stopped halfway up the steps. For a split second he paused, as if he was gathering his patience, then turned back to her. His jaw was set but his face was carefully blank.

'If you insist.'

He held it out to her. He was standing two steps higher than she was, and Sophie had to tilt her head back to look up at him. Thrown for a second by the expression in his hooded eyes, she reached out to take the bag from him but, instead of the strap, found herself grasping his hand. She snatched hers away quickly, at exactly the same time he did, and the bag fell, tumbling down the steps, scattering all her clothes into the snow.

'Oh, knickers,' she muttered, dropping to her knees as yet another giggle of horrified, slightly hysterical amusement rose up inside her. Her heart was thumping madly from the accidental contact with him. His hand had felt warm, she thought irrationally. She'd expected it to be as cold as his personality.

'Hardly,' he remarked acidly, stooping to pick up a pink thong and tossing it back into the bag. 'But clearly what passes for them in your wardrobe. You seem to have a lot of underwear and not many clothes.'

The way he said it suggested he didn't think this was a good thing.

'Yes, well,' she said loftily, 'what's the point of spending money on clothes that I'm going to get bored of after I've worn them once? Underwear is a good investment. Because it's practical,' she added defensively, seeing the faint look of scorn on his face. 'God,' she muttered crossly, grabbing a handful of clothes back from him. 'This journey's turning into one of those awful drawing-room farces.'

Straightening up, he raised an eyebrow. 'The entire weekend is a bit of a farce, wouldn't you say?'

He went up the remainder of the steps to the door. Shoving
the escaped clothes back into her bag with unnecessary force,
Sophie followed him and was about to apologise for having
the wrong underwear and the wrong clothes and the wrong
accent and occupation and attitude when she found herself
inside the castle and her defiance crumbled into dust.

The stone walls rose to a vaulted ceiling what seemed
like miles above her head, and every inch was covered with
muskets, swords, pikes and other items of barbaric medieval
weaponry that Sophie recognised from men-in-tights-with-
swords films she'd worked on, but couldn't begin to name.
They were arranged into intricate patterns around helmets
and pieces of armour, and the light from a huge wrought-iron
lantern that hung on a chain in the centre of the room glinted
dully on their silvery surfaces.

'What a cosy and welcoming entrance,' she said faintly,
walking over to a silver breastplate hanging in front of a pair
of crossed swords. 'I bet you're not troubled by persistent
double-glazing salesmen.'

He didn't smile. His eyes, she noticed, held the same dull
metallic gleam as the armour. 'They're seventeenth century.
Intended for invading enemies rather than double-glazing
salesmen.'

'Gosh.' Sophie looked away, trailing a finger down the
hammered silver of the breastplate, noticing the shining path
it left through the dust. 'You Fitzroys must have a lot of enemies.'

She was aware of his eyes upon her. Who would have
thought that such a cool stare could make her skin feel as
if it were burning? Somewhere a clock was ticking loudly,
marking out the seconds before he replied, 'Let's just say we
protect our interests.'

His voice was dangerously soft. Sophie's heart gave a kick, as if the armour had given her an electric shock. Withdrawing her hand sharply, she jerked her head up to look at him. A faint, sardonic smile touched the corner of his mouth. 'And it's not just invading armies that threaten those.'

His meaning was clear, and so was the thinly veiled warning behind the words. Sophie opened her mouth to protest, but no words came—none that would be any use in defending herself against the accusation he was making anyway, and certainly none that would be acceptable to use to a man with whose family she was going to be a guest for the weekend.

'I-I'd better find Jasper,' she stammered. 'He'll be wondering where I am.'

He turned on his heel and she followed him through another huge hallway panelled in oak, her footsteps making a deafening racket on the stone-flagged floor. There were vast fireplaces at each end of the room, but both were empty, and Sophie noticed her breath made faint plumes in the icy air. This time, instead of weapons, the walls were hung with the glassy-eyed heads of various large and hapless animals. They seemed to stare balefully at Sophie as she passed, as if in warning.

This is what happens if you cross the Fitzroys.

Sophie straightened her shoulders and quickened her pace. She mustn't let Kit Fitzroy get to her. He had got entirely the wrong end of the stick. She was Jasper's friend and she'd come as a favour to him precisely *because* his family were too bigoted to accept him as he really was.

She would have loved to confront Kit Superior Fitzroy with that, but of course it was impossible. For Jasper's sake, and also because there was something about Kit that made her lose the ability to think logically and speak articulately, damn him.

A set of double doors opened at the far end of the hallway and Jasper appeared.

'*Soph!* You're *here!*'

At least she thought it was Jasper. Gone were the layers of eccentric vintage clothing, the tattered silk-faced dinner jackets he habitually wore over T-shirts and torn drainpipe jeans. The man who came towards her, his arms outstretched, was wearing well-ironed chinos and a V-necked jumper over a button-down shirt and—Sophie's incredulous gaze moved downwards—what looked suspiciously like brogues.

Reaching her, this new Jasper took her face between his hands and kissed her far more tenderly than normal. Caught off guard by the bewildering change in him, Sophie was just about to push him away and ask what he was playing at when she remembered what she was there for. Dropping her poor, battered bag again, she wrapped her arms around his neck.

Over Jasper's shoulder, through the curtain of her hair, she was aware of Kit Fitzroy standing like some dark sentinel, watching her. The knowledge stole down inside her, making her feel hot, tingling, restless, and before she knew it she was arching her body into Jasper's, sliding her fingers into his hair.

Sophie had done enough screen and stage kisses to have mastered the art of making something completely chaste look a whole lot more X-rated than it really was. When Jasper pulled back a little a few seconds later she caught the gleam of laughter in his eyes as he leaned his forehead briefly against hers, then, stepping away, he spoke in a tone of rather forced warmth.

'You've met my big brother, Kit. I hope he's been looking after you.'

That was rather an unfortunate way of putting it, Sophie thought, an image of Kit Fitzroy, his strong hands full of her silliest knickers and bras flashing up inside her head. Oh, hell, why did she always smirk when she was embarrassed? Biting her lip, she stared down at the stone floor.

'Oh, absolutely,' she said, nodding furiously. 'And I'm afraid I needed quite a lot of looking after. If it wasn't for Kit I'd be halfway to Edinburgh now. Or at least, my underwear would.'

It might be only a few degrees warmer than the arctic, but beneath her coat Sophie could feel the heat creeping up her cleavage and into her cheeks. The nervous smile she'd been struggling to suppress broke through as she said the word 'underwear', but one glance at Kit's glacial expression killed it instantly.

'It was a lucky coincidence that we were sitting in the same carriage. It gave us a chance to…get to know each other a little before we got here.'

Ouch.

Only Sophie could have understood the meaning behind the polite words or picked up the faint note of menace beneath the blandness of his tone.

He's really got it in for me, she realised with a shiver. Suddenly she felt very tired, very alone, and even Jasper's hand around hers couldn't dispel the chilly unease that had settled in the pit of her stomach.

'Great.' Oblivious to the tension that crackled like static in the air, Jasper pulled her impatiently forwards. 'Come and meet Ma and Pa. I haven't stopped talking about you since I got here yesterday, so they're dying to see what all the fuss is about.'

And suddenly panic swelled inside her—churning, black and horribly familiar. The fear of being looked at. Scrutinised. Judged. That people would see through the layers of her disguise, the veils of evasion, to the real girl beneath. As Jasper led her towards the doors at the far end of the hall she was shaking, assailed by the same doubts and insecurities that had paralysed her the only time she'd done live theatre, in the seconds before she went onstage. What if she couldn't do it? What if the lines wouldn't come and she was left just being herself? Acting had been a way of life long before it became a way of making a living, and playing a part was second nature to her. But now…*here*…

'Jasper,' she croaked, pulling back. 'Please—wait.'

'Sophie? What's the matter?'

His kind face was a picture of concern. The animal heads glared down at her, as well as a puffy-eyed Fitzroy ancestor with a froth of white lace around his neck.

And that was the problem. Jasper was her closest friend and she would do anything for him, but when she'd offered to help him out she hadn't reckoned on all this. Alnburgh Castle, with its history and its million symbols of wealth and status and *belonging*, was exactly the kind of place that unnerved her most.

'I can't go in there. Not dressed like this, I mean. I—I came straight from the casting for the vampire thing and I meant to get changed on the train, but I…'

She opened her coat and Jasper gave a low whistle.

'Don't worry,' he soothed. 'Here, let me take your coat and you can put this on, otherwise you'll freeze.' Quickly he peeled off the black cashmere jumper and handed it to her, then tossed her coat over the horns of a nearby stuffed stag. 'They're going to love you whatever you're wearing. Particularly Pa—you're the perfect birthday present. Come on, they're waiting in the drawing room. At least it's warm in there.'

With Kit's eyes boring into her back Sophie had no choice but to let Jasper lead her towards the huge double doors at the far end of the hall.

Vampire thing, Kit thought scornfully. Since when had the legend of the undead mentioned dressing like an escort in some private men's club? He wondered if it was going to be the kind of film the boys in his unit sometimes brought back from leave to enjoy with a lot of beer in rest periods in camp.

The thought was oddly unsettling.

Tiredness pulled at him like lead weights. He couldn't face seeing his father and stepmother just yet. Going through the hallway in the direction of the stairs, he passed the place where the portrait of his mother used to hang, before Ralph had replaced it, appropriately, with a seven-foot-high oil of Tatiana in plunging blue satin and the Cartier diamonds he had given her on their wedding day.

Jasper was right, Kit mused. If there was anyone who would appreciate Sophie Greenham's get-up it was Ralph Fitzroy. Like vampires, his father's enthusiasm for obvious women was legendary.

Jasper's, however, was not. And that was what worried him. Even if he hadn't overheard her conversation on the phone, even if he hadn't felt himself the white-hot sexuality she exuded, you only had to look at the two of them together to know that, vampire or not, the girl was going to break the poor bastard's heart and eat it for breakfast.

The room Jasper led her into was as big as the last, but stuffed with furniture and blazing with light from silk-shaded lamps on every table, a chandelier the size of a spaceship hovering above a pair of gargantuan sofas and a fire roaring in the fireplace.

It was Ralph Fitzroy who stepped forwards first. Sophie was surprised by how old he was, which she realised was ridiculous considering the reason she had come up this weekend was to attend his seventieth birthday party. His grey hair was brushed back from a florid, fleshy face and as he took Sophie's hand his eyes almost disappeared in a fan of laughter lines as they travelled down her body. And up again, but only as far as her chest.

'Sophie. Marvellous to meet you,' he said, in the kind of upper-class accent that Sophie had thought had become extinct after the war.

'And you, sir.'

Oh, for God's sake—*sir*? Where had that come from? She'd be bobbing curtsies next. She was supposed to be playing the part of Jasper's girlfriend, not the parlourmaid in some nineteen-thirties below-stairs drama. Not that Ralph seemed to mind. He was still clasping her hand, looking at her with a kind of speculative interest, as if she were a piece of art he was thinking of buying.

Suddenly she remembered Jean-Claude's 'Nude with Lilies' and felt pins and needles of embarrassment prickle her whole body. Luckily distraction came in the form of a woman unfolding herself from one of the overstuffed sofas and coming forwards. She was dressed immaculately in a clinging off-white angora dress that was cleverly designed to showcase her blonde hair and peachy skin, as well as her enviable figure and the triple string of pearls around her neck. Taking hold of Sophie's shoulders, she leaned forwards in a waft of expensive perfume and, in a silent and elaborate pantomime, kissed the air beside first one cheek and then the other.

'Sophie, how good of you to come all this way to join us. Did you have a dreadful journey?'

Her voice still bore the unmistakable traces of a Russian accent, but her English was so precise that Sophie felt more than ever that they were onstage and reciting lines from a script. Tatiana Fitzroy was playing the part of the gracious hostess, thrilled to be meeting her adored son's girlfriend for the first time. The problem was she wasn't that great at acting.

'No, not at all.'

'But you came by train?' Tatiana shuddered slightly. 'Trains are always so overcrowded these days. They make one feel slightly grubby, don't you think?'

No, Sophie wanted to say. Trains didn't make her feel remotely grubby. However, the blatant disapproval in Kit Fitzroy's cool glare—now that had definitely left her feeling in need of a scrub down in a hot shower.

'Come on, darling,' Ralph joked. 'When was the last time you went on a train?'

'First Class isn't *too* bad,' Sophie said, attempting to sound as if she would never consider venturing into standard.

'Not really enough legroom,' said a grave voice behind her. Sophie whipped her head round. Kit was standing in the doorway, holding a bundle of envelopes, which he was scanning through as he spoke.

The fire crackled merrily away, but Sophie was aware that the temperature seemed to have fallen a couple of degrees. For a split second no one moved, but then Tatiana was moving forwards, as if the offstage prompt had just reminded her of her cue.

'Kit. Welcome back to Alnburgh.'

So, she wasn't the only one who found him impossible, Sophie thought, noticing the distinct coolness in Tatiana's tone. As she reached up to kiss his cheek Kit didn't incline his head even a fraction to make it easier for her to reach, and his inscrutable expression didn't alter at all.

'Tatiana. You're looking well,' Kit drawled, barely glancing at her as he continued to look through the sheaf of letters in his hand. He seemed to have been built on a different scale from Jasper and Ralph, Sophie thought, taking in his height and the breadth of his chest. The sleeves of his white shirt were rolled back to reveal tanned forearms, corded with muscle.

She looked resolutely away.

Ralph went over to a tray crowded with cut-glass decanters on a nearby table and sloshed some more whisky into a glass that wasn't quite empty. Sophie heard the rattle of glass against glass, but when he turned round to face his eldest son his bland smile was perfectly in place.

'Kit.'

'Father.'

Kit's voice was perfectly neutral, but Ralph seemed to flinch slightly. He covered it by taking a large slug of whisky. 'Good of you to come, what with flights being cancelled and so on. The invitation was…' he hesitated '…a courtesy. I know how busy you are. Hope you didn't feel obliged to accept.'

'Not at all.' Kit's eyes glittered, as cold as moonlight on frost. 'I've been away too long. And there are things we need to discuss.'

Ralph laughed, but Sophie could see the colour rising in his florid cheeks. It was fascinating—like being at a particularly tense tennis match.

'For God's sake, Kit, you're not still persisting with that—'

As he spoke the double doors opened and a thin, elderly man appeared between them and nodded, almost imperceptibly, at Tatiana. Swiftly she crossed the Turkish silk rug in a waft of Chanel No 5 and slipped a hand through her husband's arm, cutting him off mid-sentence.

'Thank you, Thomas. Dinner is ready. Now that everyone's here, shall we go through?'

CHAPTER FOUR

DINNER was about as enjoyable and relaxing as being stripped naked and whipped with birch twigs.

When she was little, Sophie had dreamed wistfully about being part of the kind of family who gathered around a big table to eat together every evening. If she'd known this was what it was like she would have stuck to the fantasies about having a pony or being picked to star in a new film version of *The Little House on the Prairie*.

The dining room was huge and gloomy, its high, green damask-covered walls hung with yet more Fitzroy ancestors. They were an unattractive bunch, Sophie thought with a shiver. The handsomeness so generously bestowed on Jasper and Kit must be a relatively recent addition to the gene pool. Only one—a woman in blush-pink silk with roses woven into her extravagantly piled up hair and a secretive smile on her lips—held any indication of the good looks that were the Fitzroy hallmark now.

Thomas, the butler who had announced dinner, dished up watery consommé, followed by tiny rectangles of grey fish on something that looked like spinach and smelled like boiled socks. No wonder Tatiana was so thin.

'This looks delicious,' Sophie lied brightly.

'Thank you,' Tatiana cooed, in a way that suggested she'd cooked it herself. 'It has taken years to get Mrs Daniels to cook things other than steak and kidney pudding and roast beef, but finally she seems to understand the meaning of low-fat.'

'Unfortunately,' Kit murmured.

Ignoring him, Ralph reached for the dusty bottle of Chateau Marbuzet and splashed a liberal amount into his glass before turning to fill up Sophie's.

'So, Jasper said you've been in Paris? Acting in some film or other?'

Sophie, who had just taken a mouthful of fish, could only nod.

'Fascinating,' said Tatiana doubtfully. 'What was it about?'

Sophie covered her mouth with her hand to hide the grimace as she swallowed the fish. 'It's about British Special Agents and the French Resistance in the Second World War,' she said, wondering if she could hide the rest of the fish under the spinach as she used to do at boarding school. 'It's set in Montmartre, against a community of painters and poets.'

'And what part did you play?'

Sophie groaned inwardly. It would have to be Kit who asked that. Ever since she sat down she'd been aware of his eyes on her. More than aware of it—it felt as if there were a laser trained on her skin.

She cleared her throat. 'Just a tiny role, really,' she said with an air of finality.

'As?'

He didn't give up, did he? Why didn't he just go the whole hog and whip out a megawatt torch to shine in her face while he interrogated her? Not that those silvery eyes weren't hard enough to look into already.

'A prostitute called Claudine who inadvertently betrays her Resistance lover to the SS.'

Kit's smile was as faint as it was fleeting. He had a way of making her feel like a third year who'd been caught showing her knickers behind the bike sheds and hauled into the headmaster's office. She took a swig of wine.

'You must meet such fascinating people,' Tatiana said.

'Oh, yes. Well, I mean, sometimes. Actors can be a pretty self-obsessed bunch. They're not always a laugh a minute to be around.'

'Not as bad as artists,' Jasper chipped in absently as he concentrated on extracting a bone from his fish. 'They hired a few painters to produce the pictures that featured in the film, and they turned out to be such prima donnas they made the actors look very down-to-earth, didn't they, Soph?'

Somewhere in the back of Sophie's mind an alarm bell had started drilling. She looked up, desperately trying to telegraph warning signals across the table to Jasper, but he was still absorbed in exhuming the skeleton of the poor fish. Sophie's lips parted in wordless panic as she desperately tried to think of something to say to steer the subject onto safer ground…

Too late.

'One of them became completely obsessed with painting Sophie,' Jasper continued. 'He came over to her in the bar one evening when I was there and spent about two hours gazing at her with his eyes narrowed as he muttered about lilies.'

Sophie felt as if she'd been struck by lightning, a terrible rictus smile still fixed to her face. She didn't dare look at Kit. She didn't need to—she could feel the disapproval and hostility radiating from him like a force field. Through her despair she was aware of the woman with the roses in her hair staring down at her from the portrait. Now the smile didn't look secretive so much as if she was trying not to laugh.

'If I thought the result would have been as lovely as that I would have accepted like a shot,' she said in a strangled voice, gesturing up at the portrait. 'Who is she?'

Ralph followed her gaze. 'Ah—that's Lady Caroline, wife of the fourth Earl and one of the more flamboyant Fitzroys.

She was a girl of somewhat uncertain provenance who had been a music hall singer—definitely not countess material. Christopher Fitzroy was twenty years younger than her, but from the moment he met her he was quite besotted and, much to the horror of polite society, married her.'

'That was pretty brave of him,' Sophie said, relief at having successfully moved the conversation on clearly audible in her voice.

The sound Kit made was unmistakably derisive. 'Brave, or stupid?'

Their eyes met. Suddenly the room seemed very quiet. The arctic air was charged with electricity, so that the candle flames flickered for a second.

'Brave,' she retorted, raising her chin a little. 'It can't have been easy, going against his family and society, but if he loved her it would have been worth the sacrifice.'

'Not if *she* wasn't worth the sacrifice.'

The candle flames danced in a halo of red mist before Sophie's eyes, and before she could stop herself she heard herself give a taut, brittle laugh and say, 'Why? Because she was too *common*?'

'Not at all.' Kit looked at her steadily, his haughty face impassive. 'She wasn't worth it because she didn't love him back.'

'How do you know she didn't?'

Oh, jeez, what was she doing? She was supposed to be here to impress Jasper's family, not pick fights with them. No matter how insufferable they were.

'Well…' Kit said thoughtfully. 'The fact that she slept with countless other men during their marriage is a bit of a clue, wouldn't you say? Her lovers included several footmen and stable lads and even the French artist who painted that portrait.'

He was still looking at her. His voice held that now-familiar note of scorn, but was so soft that for a moment Sophie was hypnotised. The candlelight cast shadows under his angular cheekbones and brought warmth to his skin, but nothing could melt the ice chips in his eyes.

Sophie jumped slightly as Ralph cut in.

'French? Thought the chap was Italian?'

Kit looked away. 'Ah, yes,' he said blandly. 'I must be getting my facts mixed up.'

Bastard, thought Sophie. He knew that all along, and he was just trying to wind her up. Raising her chin and summoning a smile to show she wouldn't be wound, she said, 'So—what happened to her?'

'She came to a sticky end, I'm afraid. Not nice,' Ralph answered, topping up his glass again and emptying the remains of the bottle into Sophie's. Despite the cold his cheeks were flushed a deep, mottled purple.

'How?' Her mind flashed back to the swords and muskets in the entrance hall, the animal heads on the wall. You messed with a Fitzroy—or his brother—and a sticky end was pretty inevitable.

'She got pregnant,' Kit said matter-of-factly, picking up the knife on his side-plate and examining the tarnished silver blade for a second before polishing it with his damask napkin. 'The Earl, poor bastard, was delighted. At last, a long-awaited heir for Alnburgh.'

Sophie took another mouthful of velvety wine, watching his mouth as he spoke. And then found that she couldn't stop watching it. And wondering what it would look like if he smiled—really smiled. Or laughed. What it would feel like if he kissed her—

No. *Stop.* She shouldn't have let Ralph give her the rest of that wine. Hastily she put her glass down and tucked her hands under her thighs.

'But of course, she knew that it was extremely unlikely

the kid was his,' Kit was saying in his low, slightly scorn-ful voice. 'And though he was too besotted to see what was going on, the rest of his family certainly weren't. She must have realised that she'd reached a dead end, and also that the child was likely to be born with the rampant syphilis that was already devouring her.'

Sophie swallowed. 'What did she do?'

Kit laid the knife down and looked straight at her. 'In the last few weeks of her pregnancy, she threw herself off the battlements in the East Tower.'

She wouldn't let him see that he'd shocked her. Wouldn't let the sickening feeling she had in the pit of her stomach show on her face. Luckily at that moment Jasper spoke, his cheerful voice breaking the tension that seemed to shiver in the icy air.

'Poor old Caroline, eh? What a price to pay for all that fun.' He leaned forwards, dropping his voice theatrically. 'It's said that on cold winter nights her ghost walks the walls, half mad with guilt. Or maybe it's the syphilis—that's supposed to make you go mad, isn't it?'

'Really, Jasper. I think we've heard enough about Fitzroys.' Tatiana laid down her napkin with a little pout as Thomas re-appeared to collect up the plates. 'So, Sophie—tell us about *your* family. Where do your people come from?'

People? Her *people*? She made it sound as if everyone had estates and villages and hordes of peasants at their command. From behind Tatiana's head Caroline the feckless countess looked at Sophie with amused pity. *Get yourself out of this one*, she seemed to say.

'Oh. Um, down in the south of England,' Sophie muttered vaguely, glancing at Jasper for help. 'We travelled around a lot, actually.'

'And your parents—what do they do?'

'My mother is an astronomer.'

It was hardly a lie, more a slip of the tongue. Astronomy/ astrology…people got them mixed up all the time anyway.

'And your—'

Jasper came swiftly to the rescue.

'Talking of stars, how did your big charity auction go last week, Ma? I keep meaning to ask you who won the premiere tickets I donated.'

It wasn't the most subtle of conversational diversions, but it did the trick so Sophie was too relieved to care. As the discussion moved on and Thomas reappeared to clear the table she slumped back in her chair and breathed out slowly, waiting for her heartbeat to steady and her fight-or-flight response to subside. With any luck that was the subject of her family dealt with and now she could relax for the rest of the weekend.

If it were possible to relax with Kit Fitzroy around.

Before she was aware it was happening or could stop it her gaze had slid back to where he sat, leaning back in his chair, his broad shoulders and long body making the antique rosewood look as fussy and flimsy as doll's-house furniture. His face was shuttered, his hooded eyes downcast, so that for the first time since the train she was able to look at him properly.

A shiver of sexual awareness shimmered down her spine and spread heat into her pelvis.

Sophie had an unfortunate attraction to men who were bad news. Men who didn't roll over and beg to be patted. But even she had to draw a line somewhere, and 'emotion-bypass' was probably a good place. And after the carnage of her so-called casual fling with Jean-Claude, this was probably a good time.

'…really fabulous turnout. People were so generous,' Tatiana was saying in her guttural purr, the diamonds in her rings glittering in the candlelight as she folded her hands together and rested her chin on them. 'And so good to catch up with all the people I don't see, stuck out here. As a matter of fact, Kit—your name came up over dinner. A girlfriend of mine said you have broken the heart of a friend of her daughter's.'

Kit looked up.

'Without the name of the friend, her daughter or her daughter's friend I can't really confirm or deny that.'

'Oh, come on,' Tatiana said with a brittle, tinkling laugh. 'How many hearts have you broken recently? I'm talking about Alexia. According to Sally Rothwell-Hyde, the poor girl is terribly upset.'

'I'm sure Sally Rothwell-Hyde is exaggerating,' Kit said in a bored voice. 'Alexia was well aware from the start it was nothing serious. It seems that Jasper will be providing Alnburgh heirs a lot sooner than I will.'

He looked across at Sophie, wondering what smart response she would think up to that, but she said nothing. She was sitting very straight, very still. Against the vivid red of her hair, her face was the same colour as the wax that had dripped onto the table in front of her.

'Something wrong?' he challenged quietly.

She looked at him, and for a second the expression in her eyes was one of blank horror. But then she blinked, and seemed to rouse herself.

'I'm sorry. What was that?' With an unsteady hand she stroked her hair back from her face. It was still as pale as milk, apart from a blossoming of red on each cheekbone.

'Soph?' Jasper got to his feet. 'Are you OK?'

'Yes. Yes, of course. I'm absolutely fine.' She made an attempt at a laugh, but Kit could hear the raw edge in it. 'Just tired, that's all. It's been a long day.'

'Then you must get to bed,' Tatiana spoke with an air of finality, as if she was dismissing her. 'Jasper, show Sophie to her room. I'm sure she'll feel much better after a good night's sleep.'

Kit watched Jasper put his arm round her and lead her to the door, remembering the two hours of catatonic sleep she'd had on the train. Picking up his wine glass, he drained it thoughtfully.

It certainly wasn't tiredness that had drained her face of colour like that, which meant it must have been the idea of producing heirs.

It looked as if she was beginning to get an idea of what she'd got herself into. And she was even flakier than he'd first thought.

CHAPTER FIVE

ROTHWELL-HYDE.

Wordlessly Sophie let Jasper lead her up the widest staircase she'd ever seen. It was probably a really common surname, she thought numbly. The phone book must contain millions of Rothwell-Hydes. Or several anyway, in smart places all over the country. Because surely no one who lived up here would send their daughter to school down in Kent?

It was a second before she realised Jasper had stopped at the foot of another small flight of stairs leading to a gloomy wood-panelled corridor with a single door at the end.

'Your room's at the end there, but let's go to mine. The fire's lit, and I've got a bottle of Smirnoff that Sergio gave me somewhere.' He took hold of her shoulders, bending his knees slightly to peer into her face. 'You look like you could do with something to revive you, angel. Are you OK?'

With some effort she gathered herself and made a stab at sounding casual and reassuring. 'I'm fine now, really. I'm so sorry, Jasper—I'm supposed to be taking the pressure off you by posing as your girlfriend, but instead your parents must be wondering why you ended up going out with such a nutter.'

'Don't be daft. You're totally charming them—or you were until you nearly fainted face down on your plate. I know the fish was revolting, but really...'

She laughed. 'It wasn't that bad.'

'What then?'

Jasper was her best friend. Over the years she'd told him lots of funny stories about her childhood, and when you'd grown up living in a converted bus painted with flowers and peace slogans, with a mother who had inch-long purple hair, had changed her name to Rainbow and given up wearing a bra, there were lots of those.

There were also lots of bits that weren't funny at all, but she kept those to herself. The years when she'd been taken in by Aunt Janet and had been sent to an exclusive girls' boarding school in the hope of 'civilising' her. Years when she'd been at the mercy of Olympia Rothwell-Hyde and her friends...

She shook her head and smiled. 'Just tired. Honest.'

'Come on, then.' He set off again along the corridor, rubbing his arms vigorously. 'God, if you stand still for a second in this place you run the risk of turning into a pillar of ice. I hope you brought your thermal underwear.'

'Please, can you not mention underwear,' Sophie said with a bleak laugh. 'The contents of my knicker drawer have played far too much of a starring role in this weekend already and I've only been here a couple of hours.' Her heart lurched as she remembered again the phone conversation Kit had overheard on the train. 'I'm afraid I got off on completely the wrong foot with your brother.'

'Half-brother,' Jasper corrected, bitterly. 'And don't worry about Kit. He doesn't approve of anyone. He just sits in judgment on the rest of us.'

'That's why I'm here, isn't it?' said Sophie. 'It's Kit's opinion you're worried about, not your parents'.'

'Are you kidding?' Jasper said ironically. 'You've met my father. He's from the generation and background that call gay men "nancy boys" and assume they all wear pink scarves and carry handbags.'

'And what's Kit's excuse?'

Pausing in front of a closed door, Jasper bowed his head. Without the hair gel and eyeliner he always wore in London his fine-boned face looked younger and oddly vulnerable.

'Kit's never liked me. I've always known that, growing up. He never said anything unkind or did anything horrible to me, but he didn't have to. I always felt this...*coldness* from him, which was almost worse.'

Sophie could identify with that.

'I don't know,' he went on, 'now I'm older I can understand that it must have been difficult for him, growing up without his mother when I still had mine.' He cast her a rueful look. 'As you'll have noticed, my mother isn't exactly cosy—I don't think she particularly went out of her way to make sure he was OK, but because I was her only child I did get rather spoiled, I guess...'

Sophie widened her eyes. 'You? Surely not!'

Jasper grinned. 'This is the part of the castle that's supposed to be haunted by the mad countess's ghost, you know, so you'd better watch it, or I'll run away and leave you here...'

'Don't you dare!'

Laughing, he opened the door. 'This is my room. Damn, the fire's gone out. Come in and shut the door to keep any lingering traces of warmth in.'

Sophie did as she was told. The room was huge, and filled with the kind of dark, heavy furniture that looked as if it had come from a giant's house. A sleigh bed roughly the size of the bus that had formed Sophie's childhood home stood in the centre of the room, piled high with several duvets. Jasper's personal stamp was evident in the tatty posters on the walls, a polystyrene reproduction of Michelangelo's *David*, which was rakishly draped in an old school tie, a silk dressing gown and a battered trilby. As he poked at the ashes in the grate

Sophie picked her way through the clothes on the floor and went over to the window.

'So what happened to Kit's mother?'

Jasper piled coal into the grate. 'She left. When he was about six, I think. It's a bit of a taboo subject around here, but I gather there was no warning, no explanation, no good-bye. Of course there was a divorce eventually, and apparently Juliet's adultery was cited, but as far as I know Kit never had any contact with her again.'

Outside it had stopped snowing and the clouds had parted to show the flat disc of the full moon. From what Sophie could see, Jasper's room looked down over some kind of inner courtyard. The castle walls rose up on all sides—battlements like jagged teeth, stone walls gleaming like pewter in the cold, bluish light. She shivered, her throat constricting with reluctant compassion for the little boy whose mother had left him here in this bleak fortress of a home.

'So she abandoned him to go off with another man?'

Sophie's own upbringing had been unconventional enough for her not to be easily shocked. But a mother leaving her child…

'Pretty much. So I guess you can understand why he ended up being like he is. Ah, look—that's better.'

He stood back, hands on hips, his face bathed in orange as the flames took hold. 'Right—let's find that bottle and get under the duvet. You can tell me all about Paris and how you managed to escape the clutches of that lunatic painter, and in turn I'm going to bore you senseless talking about Sergio. Do you know,' he sighed happily, 'he's having a tally of the days we're apart tattooed on his chest?'

The ancient stones on top of the parapet were worn smooth by salt wind and wild weather, and the moonlight turned them to beaten silver. Kit exhaled a cloud of frozen air, propping his elbows on the stone and looking out across the battlements to the empty beach beyond.

There was no point in even trying to get to sleep tonight, he knew that. His insomnia was always at its worst when he'd just come back from a period of active duty and his body hadn't learned to switch off from its state of high alert. The fact that he was also back at Alnburgh made sleep doubly unlikely.

He straightened up, shoving his frozen fingers into his pockets. The tide was out and pools of water on the sand gleamed like mercury. In the distance the moon was reflected without a ripple in the dark surface of the sea.

It was bitterly cold.

Long months in the desert halfway across the world had made him forget the aching cold here. Sometimes, working in temperatures of fifty degrees wearing eighty pounds of explosive-proof kit, he would try to recapture the sensation, but out there cold became an abstract concept. Something you knew about in theory, but couldn't imagine actually *feeling*.

But it was real enough now, as was the complicated mix of emotions he always experienced when he returned. He did one of the most dangerous jobs on the planet without feeling anything, and yet when he came back to the place he'd grown up in it was as if he'd had a layer of skin removed. Here it was impossible to forget the mother who had left him, or forgive the studied indifference of the father who had been left to bring him up. Here everything was magnified: bitterness, anger, frustration...

Desire.

The thought crept up on him and he shoved it away. Sophie Greenham was hardly his type, although he had to admit that doing battle with her at dinner had livened up what would otherwise have been a dismal evening. And at least her presence had meant that he didn't feel like the only outsider.

It had also provided a distraction from the tension between him and his father. But only temporarily. Ralph was
right—Kit hadn't come up here because the party invitation
was too thrilling to refuse, but Ralph's seventieth birthday
seemed like a good time to remind his father that if he didn't
transfer the ownership of Alnburgh into Kit's name soon, it
would be too late. The estate couldn't possibly survive the
inheritance tax that would be liable on it after Ralph's death,
and would no doubt have to be sold.

Kit felt fresh anger bloom inside him. He wasn't sure why
he cared—his house in Chelsea was conveniently placed for
some excellent restaurants, was within easy taxi-hailing range
for women he didn't want to wake up with, and came without ghosts. And yet he did care. Because of the waste and
the irresponsibility and the sheer bloody shortsightedness,
perhaps? Or because he could still hear his mother's voice,
whispering to him down the years?

*Alnburgh is yours, Kit. Don't ever forget that. Don't ever
let anyone tell you it's not.*

It must have been just before she left that she'd said that.
When she knew she was going and wanted to assuage her
guilt; to feel that she wasn't leaving him with nothing.

As if a building could make up for a mother. Particularly a
building like Alnburgh. It was an anachronism. As a home it
was uncomfortable, impractical and unsustainable. It was also
the place where he had been unhappiest. And yet he knew,
deep down, that it mattered to him. He felt responsible for it,
and he would do all he could to look after it.

And much as it surprised him to discover, that went for his
brother too. Only Jasper wasn't at risk from dry rot or damp,
but the attentions of a particularly brazen redhead.

Kit wondered if she'd be as difficult to get rid of.

* * *

Sophie opened her eyes.

It was cold and for a moment her sleep-slow brain groped to work out where she was. It was a familiar feeling—one she'd experienced often as a child when her mother had been in one of her restless phases, but for some reason now it was accompanied by a sinking sensation.

Putting a hand to her head, she struggled upright. In the corner of the room the television was playing quietly to itself, and Jasper's body was warm beside her, a T-shirt of Sergio's clasped in one hand, the half-empty bottle of vodka in the other. He had fallen asleep sprawled diagonally across the bed with his head thrown back, and something about the way the lamplight fell on his face—or maybe the shuttered blankness sleep had lent it—reminded her of Kit.

Fragments of the evening reassembled themselves in her aching head. She got up, rubbing a hand across her eyes, and carefully removed the bottle from Jasper's hand. Much as she loved him, right now all she wanted was a bed to herself and a few hours of peaceful oblivion.

Tiptoeing to the door, she opened it quietly. Out in the corridor the temperature was arctic and the only light came from the moon, lying in bleached slabs on the smooth oak floorboards. Shivering, Sophie hesitated, wondering whether to go back into Jasper's room after all, but the throbbing in her head was more intense now and she thought longingly of the paracetamol in her washbag.

There was nothing for it but to brave the cold and the dark.

Her heart began to pound as she slipped quickly between the squares of silver moonlight, along the corridor and down a spiralling flight of stone stairs. Shadows engulfed her. It was very quiet. Too quiet. To Sophie, used to thin-walled apartments, bed and breakfasts, buses and camper vans on makeshift sites where someone was always strumming a guitar or playing indie-acid-trance, the silence was unnatural.

Oppressive. It buzzed in her ears, filling her head with whistling, like interference on a badly tuned radio.

She stopped, her chest rising and falling rapidly as she looked around.

Passageways stretched away from her in three directions, but each looked as unfamiliar as the other. Oh, hell. She'd been so traumatised earlier that she hadn't paid attention to Jasper when he pointed out her room…

But that could be it, she thought with relief, walking quickly to a door at the end of the short landing to her left. Gingerly she turned the handle and, heart bursting, pushed open the door.

Moonlight flooded in from behind her, illuminating the ghostly outlines of shrouded furniture. The air was stale with age. The room clearly hadn't been opened in years.

This is the part of the castle that's supposed to be haunted by the mad countess's ghost, you know…

Retreating quickly, she slammed the door and forced herself to exhale slowly. It was fine. No need to panic. Just a question of retracing her steps, thinking about it logically. A veil of cloud slipped over the moon's pale face and the darkness deepened. Icy drafts eddied around Sophie's ankles, and the edge of a curtain at one of the stone windows lifted slightly, as if brushed by invisible fingers. The whistling sound was louder now and more distinctive—a sort of keening that was almost human. She couldn't be sure it was just in her head any more and she broke into a run, glancing back over her shoulder as if she expected to see a swish of pink silk skirt disappearing around the corner.

'I'm being stupid,' she whispered desperately, fumbling at the buttons of her mobile phone to make the screen light up and act as a torch. 'There's no such thing as ghosts.' But even as the words formed themselves on her stiff lips horror prickled at the back of her neck.

Footsteps.

She clamped a hand to her mouth to stifle her moan of terror and stood perfectly still. Probably she'd imagined it—or possibly it was just the mad drumming of her heart echoing off the stone walls...

Nope. Definitely footsteps.

Definitely getting nearer.

It was impossible to tell from which direction they were coming. Or maybe if they were ghostly footsteps they weren't coming from any particular direction, except beyond the grave? It hardly mattered—the main thing was to get away from here and back to Jasper. Back to light and warmth and TV and company. Shaking with fear, she darted back along the corridor, heading for the stairs that she had come down a few moments ago.

And then she gave a whimper of horror, icy adrenaline sluicing through her veins. A dark figure loomed in front of her, only a foot or so away, too close even for her to be aware of anything beyond its height and the frightening breadth of its shoulders. She shrank backwards, bringing her hands up to her face, her mouth opening to let out the scream that was rising in her throat.

'Oh, no, you don't...'

Instantly she was pulled against the rock-hard chest and a huge hand was put across her mouth. Fury replaced fear as she realised that this was not the phantom figure of some seventeenth-century suitor looking for the countess, but the all-too-human flesh of Kit Fitzroy.

All of a sudden the idea of being assaulted by a ghost seemed relatively appealing.

'Get *off* me!' she snapped. Or tried to. The sound she actually made was a muffled, undignified squawk, but he must have understood her meaning because he let her go immediately, thrusting her away from his body as if she were contaminated. Shaking back her hair, Sophie glared at him, trying to gather some shreds of dignity. Not easy when she'd just been caught behaving like a histrionic schoolgirl because she thought he was a ghost.

'What do you think you're *doing*?' she demanded.

His arched brows rose a fraction, but other than that his stony expression didn't change. 'I'd have thought it was obvious. Stopping you from screaming and waking up the entire castle,' he drawled. 'Is Jasper aware that you're roaming around the corridors in the middle of the night?'

'Jasper's asleep.'

'Ah. Of course.' His hooded gaze didn't leave hers, but she jumped as she felt his fingers close around her wrist, like bands of iron, and he lifted the hand in which her mobile phone was clasped. His touch was as cold and hard as his tone. 'Don't tell me, you got lost on the way to the bathroom and you were using the GPS to find it?'

'No.' Sophie spoke through clenched teeth. 'I got lost on the way to my bedroom. Now, if you'd just point me in the right—'

'*Your* bedroom?' He dropped her wrist and stepped away. 'Well, it definitely won't be here. The rooms in this part of the castle haven't been used for years. But why the hell aren't you sharing with Jasper? Or perhaps you prefer to have your own…*privacy*?'

He was so tall that she had to tilt her head back to look at his face. The place where they were standing was dark and it was half in shadow, but, even so, she didn't miss the faint sneer that accompanied the word.

'I just thought it wouldn't be appropriate to sleep with Jasper in his parents' house, that's all,' she retorted haughtily. 'It didn't feel right.'

'You do a passable impression of indignant respectability,' he said in a bored voice, turning round and beginning to walk away from her down the corridor. 'But unfortunately it's rather wasted on me. I know exactly why you want your own bedroom, and it has nothing to do with propriety and everything to do with the fact that you're far from in love with my brother.'

It was those words that did it. *My brother.* Until then she had been determined to remain calm in the face of Kit Fitzroy's towering arrogance; his misguided certainty and his infuriating, undeniable sexual magnetism. Now something snapped inside her.

'No. You're *wrong,*' she spat.

'Really?' he drawled, turning to go back along the passageway down which she'd just come.

'Yes!'

Who the hell was he to judge? If it wasn't for him Jasper wouldn't have had to ask her here in the first place, to make himself look 'acceptable' in the contemptuous eyes of his brother.

Well, she couldn't explain anything without giving Jasper away, but she didn't have to take it either. Following him she could feel the pulse jumping in her wrist, in the place where his fingers had touched her, as fresh adrenaline scorched through her veins.

'I know you think the worst of me and I can understand why, but I just want to say that it wasn't—*isn't*—what you think. I would *never* hurt Jasper, or mess him around. He's the person I care most about in the world.'

He went up a short flight of steps into the corridor Sophie now remembered, and stopped in front of the door at the end.

'You have a funny way of showing it,' he said, very softly. 'By sleeping with another man.'

He opened the door and stood back for her to pass. She didn't move. 'It's not like that,' she said in a low voice. 'You don't know the whole story.'

Kit shook his head. 'I don't need to.'

Because what was there to know? He'd seen it all count-less times before—men returning back to base from leave, white-lipped and silent as they pulled down pictures of smiling wives or girlfriends from their lockers. Wives they thought they could trust while they were away. Girlfriends they thought would wait for them. Behind every betrayal there was a story, but in the end it was still a betrayal.

Folding her arms tightly across her body, she walked past him into the small room and stood by the bed with her back to him. Her hair was tangled, reminding him that she'd just left his brother's bed. In the thin, cold moonlight it gleamed like hot embers beneath the ashes of a dying fire.

'Is it common practice in the army to condemn without trial and without knowing the facts?' she asked, turning round to face him. 'You barely even *know* Jasper. You did your best to deny his existence when he was growing up, and you're not exactly going out of your way to make up for it now, so please don't lecture me about not loving him.'

'That's *enough*.'

The words were raw, razor-sharp, spoken in the split sec-ond before his automatic defences kicked in and the shutters came down on his emotions. Deliberately Kit unfurled his fists and kept his breathing steady.

'If you think finding your way around the castle is con-fusing I wouldn't even try to unravel the relationships within this family if I were you,' he said quietly. 'Don't get involved in things you don't need to understand.'

'Why? Because I won't be around long enough?' she de-manded, coming closer to him again.

Kit stiffened as he caught the scent of her again—warm, spicy, delicious. He turned away, reaching for the door handle. 'Goodnight. I hope you have everything you need.'

He shut the door and stood back from it, waiting for the

adrenaline rush to subside a little. Funny how he could work a field strewn with hidden mines, approach a car loaded with explosives and not feel anything, and yet five feet five of lying redhead had almost made him lose control.

He hated deception—too much of his childhood had been spent not knowing what to believe or who to trust—and as an actress, he supposed, Sophie Greenham was quite literally a professional in the art.

But unluckily for her he was a professional too, and there was more than one way of making safe an incendiary device. Sometimes you had to approach the problem laterally. If she wouldn't admit that her feelings for Jasper were a sham, he'd just have to prove it another way.

CHAPTER SIX

SOPHIE felt as if she'd only just fallen asleep when a knock at the door jolted her awake again. Jasper appeared, grinning sheepishly and carrying a plate of toast in one hand and two mugs of coffee in the other, some of which slopped onto the carpet as he elbowed the door shut again.

'What time is it?' she moaned, dropping back onto the pillows.

Jasper put the mugs down on the bedside table and perched on the bed beside her. 'Nearly ten. Kit said he'd bumped into you in the middle of the night trying to find your room, so I thought I'd better not wake you. You've slept for Britain.'

Sophie didn't have the heart to tell him she'd been awake most of the night, partly because she'd been frozen, partly because she'd been so hyped up with indignation and fury and the after-effects of what felt like an explosion in the sexual-chemistry lab that sleep had been a very long time coming.

He picked up a mug and looked at her through the wreaths of steam that were curling through the frigid air. 'Sorry for leaving you to wander like that. Just as well you bumped into Kit.'

Sophie grunted crossly. 'Do you think so? I thought he was the ghost of the nymphomaniac countess. No such luck.'

Jasper winced. 'He didn't give you a hard time, did he?'

'He thought it was extremely odd that we weren't sharing

a room.' Sophie reached for a coffee, more to warm her hands on than anything. 'I'm not exactly convincing him in my role as your girlfriend, you know. The thing is, he overheard me talking to Jean-Claude on the train and now he thinks I'm a two-timing trollop.'

'Oops.' Jasper took another sip of coffee while he digested this information. 'OK, well, that is a bit unfortunate, but don't worry—we still have time to turn it around at the party to-night. You'll be every man's idea of the perfect girlfriend.'

Sophie raised an eyebrow. 'In public? In front of your parents? From my experience of what men consider the perfect girlfriend, that wouldn't be wise.'

'Wicked girl,' Jasper scolded. 'I meant demure, devoted, hanging on my every word—that sort of thing. What did you bring to wear?'

'My Chinese silk dress.'

With a firm shake of his head Jasper put down his mug. 'Absolutely *not*. Far too sexy. No, what we need is something a little more…understated. A little more *modest*.'

Sophie narrowed her eyes. 'You mean frumpy, don't you? Do you have something in mind?'

Getting up, Jasper went over to the window and drew back the curtains with a theatrical flourish. 'Not something, some*where*. Get up, Cinderella, and let's hit the shops of Hawksworth.'

Jasper drove Ralph's four-by-four along roads that had been turned into ice rinks. It was a deceptively beautiful day. The sun shone in a sky of bright, hard blue and made the fields and hedgerows glitter as if each twig and blade of grass was encrusted with Swarovski crystals. He had pinched a navy-blue quilted jacket of Tatiana's to lend to Sophie, instead of the military-style overcoat of which Kit had been so scathing. Squinting at her barefaced reflection in the drop-down mir-

ror on the sun visor, she remarked that all that was missing
was a silk headscarf and her new posh-girl image would be
complete. Jasper leaned over and pulled one out of the glove
compartment. She tied it under her chin and they roared with
laughter.

They parked in the market square in the centre of a town
that looked as if it hadn't altered much in the last seventy
years. Crunching over gritted cobblestones, Jasper led her
past greengrocers, butchers and shops selling gate hinges
and sheep dip, to an ornately fronted department store. Man-
nequins wearing bad blonde wigs modelled twinsets and pat-
terned shirtwaister dresses in the windows.

'Braithwaite's—the fashion centre of the North since 1908'
read the painted sign above the door. Sophie wondered if it
was meant to be ironic.

'After you, madam,' said Jasper with a completely straight
face, holding the door open for her. 'Evening wear. First floor.'

Sophie stifled a giggle. 'I love vintage clothing, as you
know, but—'

'No buts,' said Jasper airily, striding past racks of rain-
coats towards a sweeping staircase in the centre of the store.
'Just think of it as dressing for a part. Tonight, Ms Greenham,
you are *not* going to be your gorgeous, individual but—let's
face it—slightly eccentric self. You are going to be perfect
Fitzroy-fiancée material. And that means Dull.'

At the top of the creaking staircase Sophie caught sight of
herself in a full-length mirror. In jeans and Tatiana's jacket,
the silk scarf still knotted around her neck a lurid splash of
colour against her un-made-up face, dull was exactly the
word. Still, if dull was what was required to slip beneath Kit
Fitzroy's radar that had to be a good thing.

Didn't it?

She hesitated for a second, staring into her own wide eyes,
thinking of last night and the shower of shooting stars that

had exploded inside her when he'd touched her wrist; the static that had seemed to make the air between them vibrate as they'd stood in the dark corridor. The blankness of his expression, but the way it managed to convey more vividly than a thousand well-chosen words his utter contempt...

'What do you think?'

Yes. Dull was good. The duller the better.

'Hello-*o*?'

Pasting on a smile, she turned to Jasper, who had picked out the most hideous concoction of ruffles and ruches in the kind of royal blue frequently used for school uniforms. Sophie waved her hand dismissively.

'Strictly Come Drag Queen. I thought we were going for dull—that's attention-grabbing for all the wrong reasons. No—we have to find something *really* boring...' She began rifling through rails of pastel polyester. 'We have to find the closest thing The Fashion Capital of the North has to a shroud... Here. How about this?'

Triumphantly she pulled out something in stiff black fabric—long, straight and completely unadorned. The neck was cut straight across in a way that she could imagine would make her breasts look like a sort of solid, matronly shelf, and the price tag was testament to the garment's extreme lack of appeal. It had been marked down three times already and was now almost being given away.

'Looks good to me.' Jasper flipped the hanger around, scrutinising the dress with narrowed eyes. 'Would madam like to try it on?'

'Nope. It's my size, it's horrible and it's far too cold to get undressed. Let's just buy it and go to the pub. As your fiancée I think I deserve an enormous and extremely calorific lunch.'

Jasper grinned and kissed her swiftly on the cheek. 'You're on.'

* * *

The Bull in Hawksworth was the quintessential English pub: the walls were yellow with pre-smoking-ban nicotine, a scarred dartboard hung on the wall beside an age-spotted etching of Alnburgh Castle and horse brasses were nailed to the blackened beams. Sophie slid behind a table in the corner by the fire while Jasper went to the bar. He came back with a pint of lager and a glass of red wine, and a newspaper folded under his arm.

'Food won't be a minute,' he said, taking a sip of lager, which left a froth of white on his upper lip. 'Would you mind if I gave Sergio a quick call? I brought you this to read.' He threw down the newspaper and gave her an apologetic look as he took out his phone. 'It's just it's almost impossible to get a bloody signal at Alnburgh, and I'm always terrified of being overheard anyway.'

Sophie shrugged. 'No problem. Go ahead.'

'Is there a "but" there?'

Taking a sip of her wine, she shook her head. 'No, of course not.' She put her glass down, turning the stem between her fingers. In the warmth of the fire and Jasper's familiar company she felt herself relaxing more than she had done in the last twenty-four hours. 'Except,' she went on thoughtfully, 'perhaps that I wonder if it wouldn't be easier if you came clean about all this.'

'Came out, you mean?' Jasper said with sudden weariness. 'Well, it wouldn't. It's easier just to live my own life, far away from here, without having to deal with the fallout of knowing I've let my whole family down. My father might be seventy, but he still prides himself on the reputation as a ladies' man he's spent his entire adult life building. He sees flirting with anything in a skirt as a mark of sophisticated social interaction—as you may have noticed last night. Homosexuality is utterly alien to him, so he thinks it's unnatural full stop.' With an agitated movement of his hand he knocked his pint glass so that beer splashed onto the table. 'Honestly, it would finish him off. And as for Kit—'

'Yes, well, I don't know what gives Kit the right to go around passing judgment on everyone else, like he's something special,' Sophie snapped, unfolding the paper as she moved it away from the puddle of lager on the table. 'It's not as if he's better than you because he's straight, or me because he's posh—'

'Holy cow,' spluttered Jasper, grasping her arm.

Breaking off, she followed his astonished gaze and felt the rest of the rant dissolve on her tongue. For there, on the front of the newspaper—in grainy black and white, but no less arresting for it—was Kit. Beneath the headline *Heroes Honoured* a photograph showed him in half profile, his expression characteristically blank above his dress uniform with its impressive line of medals.

Quickly, incredulously, Jasper began to read out the accompanying article.

'Major Kit Fitzroy, known as "the heart-throb hero", was awarded the George Medal for his "dedication to duty and calm, unflinching bravery in the face of extreme personal risk". Major Fitzroy has been responsible for making safe over 100 improvised explosive devices, potentially saving the lives of numerous troops and civilians, a feat which he describes as "nothing remarkable".'

For long moments neither of them spoke. Sophie felt as if she'd swallowed a firework, which was now fizzing inside her. The barmaid brought over plates of lasagne and chips and retreated again. Sophie's appetite seemed to have mysteriously deserted her.

'I suppose that does give him the right to act like he's a

bit special, and *slightly* better than you and me,' she admitted shakily. 'Did you know anything about this?'

'Not a thing.'

'But wouldn't your father want to know? Wouldn't he be pleased?'

Jasper shrugged. 'He's always been rather sneery about Kit's army career, maybe because he's of the opinion people of our class don't work, apart from in pointless, arty jobs like mine.' Picking up his pint, he frowned. 'It might also have something to do with the fact his older brother was killed in the Falklands, but I don't know. That's one of those Things We definitely Do Not Mention.'

There seemed to be quite a lot of those in the Fitzroy family, Sophie thought. She couldn't stop looking at the photograph of Kit, even though she wanted to. Or help thinking how attractive he was, even though she didn't want to.

It had been easy to write him off as an obnoxious, arrogant control-freak but what Jasper had said about his mother last night, and now this, made her see him, reluctantly, in a different light.

What was worse, it made her see herself in a different light too. Having been on the receiving end of ignorant prejudice, Sophie liked to think she would never rush to make ill-informed snap judgments about people, but she had to admit that maybe, just maybe, in this instance she had.

But so had he, she reminded herself defiantly. He had dismissed her as a shallow, tarty gold-digger when that most definitely wasn't true. The gold-digger part, anyway. Hopefully tonight, with the aid of the nunlike dress and a few pithy comments on current affairs and international politics, she'd make him see he'd been wrong about the rest too.

For Jasper's sake, obviously.

As they left she picked up the newspaper. 'Do you think they'd mind if I took this?'

'What for?' Jasper asked in surprise. 'D'you want to sleep with the heart-throb hero under your pillow?'

'No!' Annoyingly Sophie felt herself blush. 'I want to swot up on the headlines so I can make intelligent conversation tonight.'

Jasper laughed all the way back to the car.

Ralph adjusted his bow tie in the mirror above the drawing room fireplace and smoothed a hand over his brushed-back hair.

'I must say, Kit, I find your insistence on bringing up the subject of my death in rather poor taste,' he said in an aggrieved tone. 'Tonight of all nights. A milestone birthday like this is depressing enough without you reminding me constantly that the clock is ticking.'

'It's not personal,' Kit drawled, mentally noting that he'd do well to remember that himself. 'And it is boring, but the fact remains that Alnburgh won't survive the inheritance tax it'll owe on your death unless you've transferred the ownership of the estate to someone else. Seven years is the—'

Ralph cut him off with a bitter, blustering laugh. 'By someone else, I suppose you mean you? What about Jasper?'

Alnburgh is yours, Kit. Don't let anyone tell you it's not.

In the pockets of his dinner-suit trousers Kit's hands were bunched into fists. Experience had taught him that when Ralph was in this kind of punchy, belligerent mood the best way to respond was with total detachment. He wondered fleetingly if that was where he first picked up the habit.

'Jasper isn't the logical heir,' he said, very evenly.

'Oh, I don't know about that,' Ralph replied with unpleasant, mock joviality. 'Let's look at it this way—Jasper is probably going to live another sixty or seventy years, and, believe me, I have every intention of lasting a lot more than seven years. Given your job I'd say you're the one who's pushing your luck in that department, don't you think? Remember what happened to my dear brother Leo. Never came back from the Falklands. Very nasty business.'

Ralph's eyes met Kit's in the mirror and slid away. He was already well on the way to being drunk, Kit realised wearily, and that meant that any further attempt at persuasion on his part would only be counterproductive.

'Transfer it to Jasper if you want.' He shrugged, picking up the newspaper that lay folded on a coffee table. 'That would certainly be better than doing nothing, though I'm not sure he'd thank you for it since he hates being here as much as Tatiana does. It might also put him at further risk from ruthless gold-diggers like the one he's brought up this weekend.'

The medals ceremony he'd attended yesterday was front-page news. Idly he wondered whether Ralph had seen it and chosen not to say anything.

'Sophie?' Ralph turned round, putting his hands into his pockets and rocking back on the heels of his patent shoes. 'I thought she was quite charming. Gorgeous little thing, too. Good old Jasper, eh? He's got a cracker there.'

'Except for the fact that she couldn't give a toss about him,' Kit commented dryly, putting down the paper.

'Jealous, Kit?' Ralph said, and there was real malice in his tone. His eyes were narrowed, his face suddenly flushed. 'You think you're the one who should get all the good-looking girls, don't you? I'd say you want her for yourself, just like—'

At that moment the strange outburst was interrupted by Jasper coming in. Ralph broke off and turned abruptly away.

'Just like what?' Kit said softly.

'Nothing.' Ralph pulled a handkerchief from his pocket and mopped his brow. As he turned to Jasper his face lost all its hostility. 'We were just talking about you—and Sophie.'

Heading to the drinks tray, Jasper grinned. 'Gorgeous, isn't she? And really clever and talented too. Great actress.'

In his dinner suit and with his hair wet from the shower Jasper looked about fifteen, Kit thought, his heart darkening against Sophie Greenham.

'So I noticed,' he said blandly, going to the door. He turned to Ralph. 'Think about what I said about the estate transfer. Oh, and I promised Thomas I'd see to the port tonight. Any preference?'

Ralph seemed to have recovered his composure. 'There's an excellent '29. Though, on second thoughts, open some '71.' His smile held a hint of challenge. 'Let's keep the really good stuff for my hundredth, since I fully intend to be around to celebrate it.'

Crossing the portrait hall in rapid, furious strides, Kit swore with such viciousness a passing waiter shot behind a large display of flowers. So he'd failed to make Ralph see sense about the estate. He'd just have to make sure he was more successful when it came to Sophie Greenham.

It was just as well she hadn't eaten all that lasagne at lunchtime, Sophie reflected grimly, tugging at the zip on the side of the black dress. Obviously, with hindsight, trying it on in the shop would have been wise—all the croissants and baguettes in Paris must have taken more of a toll than she'd realised. Oh, well—if it didn't fit she'd just have to wear the Chinese silk that Jasper had decreed was too sexy...

Hope flared inside her. Instantly she stamped it out.

No. Tonight was not about being sexy, or having fun, she told herself sternly. Tonight was about supporting Jasper and showing Kit that she wasn't the wanton trollop he had her down as.

She thought again of the photo in the paper—unsmiling, remote, heroic—and her insides quivered a little. Because, she realised with a pang of surprise, she actually didn't want him to think that about her.

With renewed effort she gave the zip another furious tug. It shot up and she let out the lungful of air she'd been holding, looking down at the dress with a sinking heart. Her cell-like bedroom didn't boast anything as luxurious as a full-length mirror, but she didn't need to see her whole reflection to know how awful she looked. It really was the most severely unflattering garment imaginable, falling in a plain, narrow, sleeveless tube from her collarbones to her ankles. A slit up one side at least meant that she could walk without affecting tiny geishalike steps, but she felt as if she were wrapped in a roll of wartime blackout fabric.

'That's *good*,' she said out loud, giving herself a severe look in the little mirror above the sink. Her reflection stared back at her, face pale against the bright mass of her hair. She'd washed it and, gleaming under the overhead light, the colour now seemed more garish than ever. Grabbing a few pins, she stuck them in her mouth, then pulled her hair back and twisted it tightly at the back of her neck.

Standing back again, she pulled a face.

There. Disfiguring dress and headmistress hair. Jasper's dull girlfriend was ready for her public, although at least Sophie had the private satisfaction of knowing that she was also wearing very naughty underwear and what Jasper fondly called her 'shag-me' shoes. Twisting round, she tried to check the back view of the dress, and gave a snort of laughter as she noticed the price ticket hanging down between her shoulder blades.

Classy and expensive was always going to be a hard look for the girl who used to live on a bus to pull off, as Olympia Rothwell-Hyde and her cronies had never stopped reminding her. Attempting to do it with a label on her back announcing just how little she'd paid for the blackout dress would make it damned impossible.

She gave it a yank and winced as the plastic cut into her

fingers. Another try confirmed that it was definitely a job for scissors. Which she didn't have.

She bit her lip. Jasper had already gone down, telling her to join them in the drawing room as soon as she was ready, but there was no way she could face Tatiana, who would no doubt be decked out in designer finery and dripping with diamonds, with her knock-down price ticket on display. She'd just have to slip down to the kitchens and see if the terrifying Mrs Daniels—or Mrs Danvers as she'd privately named her when Jasper had introduced her this morning—had some.

The layout of the castle was more familiar now and Sophie headed for the main stairs as quickly as the narrow dress would allow. The castle felt very different this evening from the cavernous, shadowy place at which she'd arrived last night. Now the stone walls seemed to resonate with a hum of activity as teams of caterers and waiting-on staff made final preparations in the staterooms below.

It was still freezing, though. In the portrait hall the smell of woodsmoke drifted through the air, carried on icy gusts of wind that the huge fires banked in every grate couldn't seem to thaw. It mingled with the scent of hothouse flowers, which stood on every table and window ledge.

Sophie hitched up the narrow skirt of her dress and went more carefully down the narrow back stairs to the kitchens. It was noticeably warmer down here, the vaulted ceilings holding the heat from the ovens. A central stone-flagged passageway stretched beyond a row of Victorian windows in the kitchen wall, into the dimly lit distance. To the dungeons, Jasper had teased her earlier.

The dungeons, where Kit probably locked up two-timing girlfriends, she thought grimly, shivering in spite of the relative warmth. The noise of her heels echoed loudly off the stone walls. The glass between the corridor and the kitchen was clouded with steam, but through it Sophie could see that

Mrs Daniels' domain had been taken over by legions of uniformed chefs.

Of course. Jasper had mentioned that both she and Thomas the butler had been given the night off. Well, there was no way she was going in there. Turning on her high heel, she hitched up her skirt and was hurrying back in the direction she'd just come when a voice behind her stopped her in her tracks.

'Are you looking for something?'

Her heart leapt into her throat and she spun round. Kit had emerged from one of the many small rooms that led off the passageway, his shoulders, in a perfectly cut black dinner suit, seeming almost to fill the narrow space. Their eyes met, and in the harsh overhead bulk light Sophie saw him recoil slightly as a flicker of some emotion—shock, or was it distaste?—passed across his face.

'I was l-looking for M-Mrs Daniels,' she said in a strangled voice, feeling inexplicably as if he'd caught her doing something wrong again. God, no wonder he had risen so far up the ranks in the army. She'd bet he could reduce insubordinate squaddies to snivelling babies with a single glacial glare. She coughed, and continued more determinedly. 'I wanted to borrow some scissors.'

'That's a relief.' His smile was almost imperceptible. 'I assume it means I don't have to tell you that you have a price ticket hanging down your back.'

Heat prickled through her, rising up her neck in a tide of uncharacteristic shyness.

Quickly she cleared her throat again. 'No.'

'Perhaps I could help? Follow me.'

Sophie was glad of the ringing echo of her shoes on the stone floor as it masked the frantic thud of her heart. He had to duck his head to get through the low doorway and she followed him into a vaulted cellar, the brick walls of which were lined with racks of bottles that gleamed dully in the low light. There was a table on which more bottles stood, alongside a knife and stained cloth like a consumptive's handkerchief. Kit picked up the knife.

'Wh-what are you doing?'

Hypnotised, she watched him wipe the blade of the knife on the cloth.

'Decanting port.'

'What for?' she rasped, desperately trying to make some attempt at sensible conversation. Snatches of the article in the newspaper kept coming back to her, making it impossible to think clearly. *Heart-throb hero. Unflinching bravery. Extreme personal risk.* It was as if someone had taken her jigsaw puzzle image of him and broken it to bits, so the pieces made quite a different picture now.

His lips twitched into the faint half-smile she'd come to recognise, but his hooded eyes held her gravely. The coolness was still there, but they'd lost their sharp contempt.

'To get rid of the sediment. The bottle I've just opened last saw daylight over eighty years ago.'

Sophie gave a little laugh, squirming slightly under his scrutiny. 'Isn't it a bit past its sell-by date?'

'Like lots of things, it improves with age,' he said dryly, taking hold of her shoulders with surprising gentleness and turning her round. 'Would you like to try some?'

'Isn't it very expensive?'

What was it about an absence of hostility that actually made it feel like kindness? Sophie felt the hair rise on the back of her neck as his fingers brushed her bare skin. She held herself very rigid for a second, determined not to give in to the helpless shudder of desire that threatened to shake her whole body as he bent over her. Her breasts tingled, and beneath the severe lines of the dress her nipples pressed against the tight fabric.

'Put it this way, you could get several dresses like that for the price of a bottle,' he murmured, and Sophie could feel the warm whisper of his breath on her neck as he spoke. She closed her eyes, wanting the moment to stretch for ever, but then she heard the snap of plastic as he cut through the tag and he was pulling back, leaving her feeling shaky and on edge.

'To be honest, that doesn't say much about your port,' she joked weakly.

'No.' He went back over to the table and picked up a bottle, holding it up to the light for a second before pouring a little of the dark red liquid into a slender, teardrop-shaped decanter. 'It's a great dress. It suits you.'

His voice was offhand. So why did it make goosebumps rise on her skin?

'It's a very *cheap* dress.' She laughed again, awkwardly, crossing her arms across her chest to hide the obvious outline of her nipples, which had to be glaringly obvious against the plainness of the dress. 'Or is that what you meant by it suiting me?'

'No.'

He turned to face her, holding the slim neck of the decanter. She couldn't take her eyes off his hands. Against the white cuffs of his evening shirt they looked very tanned and she felt her heart twist in her chest, catching her off guard as she thought of what he had done with those hands. And what he had seen with those eyes. And now he was looking at her with that cool, dispassionate stare and she almost couldn't breathe.

'I haven't got a glass, I'm afraid.' He swirled the port around in the decanter so it gleamed like liquid rubies, and then offered it up to her lips. 'Take it slowly. Breathe it in first.'

Oh, God.

At that moment she wasn't sure she was capable of breathing at all, but it was as if he had some kind of hypnotist's hold over her and somehow she did as he said, her gaze fixed unblinkingly on his as she inhaled.

It was the scent of age and incense and reverence, and instantly she was transported back to the chapel at school, kneeling on scratchy woollen hassocks to sip communion wine and trying to ignore the whispers of Olympia Rothwell-Hyde and her friends, saying that she'd go to hell because everyone knew she hadn't even been baptised, never mind confirmed. What vicar would christen a child with a name like Summer Greenham?

She pulled away sharply just as the port touched her lips, so that it missed her mouth and dripped down her chin. Kit's reactions were like lightning—in almost the same second his hand came up to cup her face, catching the drips of priceless liquor on the palm of his hand.

'I'm sorry,' she gasped. 'I didn't mean to waste it—'

'Then let's not.'

It was just a whisper, and then he was bending his head so that, slowly, softly, his mouth grazed hers. Sophie's breathing hitched, her world stopped as his lips moved downwards to suck the drips on her chin as her lips parted helplessly and a tidal wave of lust and longing was unleashed inside her. It washed away everything, so that her head was empty of questions, doubts, uncertainties: everything except the dark, swirling whirlpool of need. Her body did the thinking, the deciding for her as it arched towards him, her hands coming up of their own volition to grip his rock-hard shoulders and tangle in his hair.

This was what she knew. This meeting of mouths and bodies, this igniting of pheromones and stoking of fires—these were feelings she understood and could deal with expertly. Familiar territory.

Or, it had been.

Not now.

Not *this*…

His touch was gentle, languid, but it seared her like a blowtorch, reducing the memory of every man who'd gone before to ashes and dust. One hand rested on her hip, the other cupped her cheek as he kissed her with a skill and a kind of brooding focus that made her tremble and melt.

And want *more*.

The stiff fabric of the hateful dress felt like armour plating. She pressed herself against him, longing to be free of it, feeling the contours of the hard muscles of his chest through the layers of clothes that separated them. Her want flared, a fire doused with petrol, and as she kissed him back her fingers found the silk bow tie at his throat, tugging at the knot, working the shirt button beneath it free.

And suddenly there was nothing gentle in the way he pulled her against him, nothing languid about the pressure of his mouth or the erotic thrust and dart of his tongue. Sophie's hands were shaking as she slid them beneath his jacket. She could feel the warmth of his body, the rapid beating of his heart as he gripped her shoulders, pushing her backwards against the ancient oak barrels behind her.

Roughly she pushed his jacket off his shoulders. His hands were at her waist and she yanked at her skirt, pulling it upwards so that he could hitch her onto a barrel. She straddled its curved surface, her hips rising to press against his, her fingers twisting in his shirt front as she struggled to pull it free of his trousers.

She was disorientated with desire. Trembling, shaking, unhinged with an urgency that went beyond anything she'd known before. The need to have him against her and in her.

'Now…please…'

She gasped as he stepped backwards, tearing his mouth

from hers, turning away. A physical sensation of loss swept through her as her hands, still outstretched towards him, reached to pull him back into her. Her breath was coming in ragged, thirsty gasps; she was unable to think of anything beyond satisfying the itch and burn that pulsed through her veins like heroin.

Until he turned back to face her again and her blood froze.

His shirt was open to the third button, his silk tie hanging loose around his neck in the classic, clichéd image from every red-blooded woman's slickest fantasy. But that was where the dream ended, because his face was like chiselled marble and his hooded eyes were as cold as ice.

And in that second, in a rush of horror and pain, Sophie understood what had just happened. What she had just done. He didn't need to say anything because his expression—completely deadpan apart from the slight curl of his lip as he looked at her across the space that separated them—said it all.

She didn't hesitate. Didn't think. It was pure instinct that propelled her across that space and made her raise her hand to slap his face.

But her instinct was no match for his reflexes. With no apparent effort at all he caught hold of her wrist and held it absolutely still for a heartbeat before letting go.

'You unutterable bastard,' she breathed.

She didn't wait for a response. Somehow she made her trembling legs carry her out of the wine cellar and along the corridor, while her horrified mind struggled to take in the enormity of what had just happened. She had betrayed Jasper and given herself away. She had proved Kit Fitzroy right. She had played straight into his hands and revealed herself as the faithless, worthless gold-digger he'd taken her for all along.

CHAPTER SEVEN

So in the end it hadn't even been as hard as he'd thought it would be.

With one quick, angry movement Kit speared the cork in another dusty bottle and twisted it out with far less care and respect than the vintage deserved.

He hadn't exactly anticipated she would be a challenge to seduce, but somehow he'd imagined a little more in the way of token resistance; some evidence of a battle with her conscience at least.

But she had responded instantly.

With a passion that matched his own.

His hand shook, and the port he was pouring through the muslin cloth into the decanter dripped like blood over the backs of his fingers. Giving a muttered curse, he put the bottle down and put his hand to his mouth to suck off the drops.

What the hell was the matter with him? His hands were usually steady as a rock—he and his entire team would have been blown to bits long ago if they weren't. And if he hesitated, or questioned himself as he was doing now...

He had done what he set out to do, and her reaction was exactly what he'd predicted.

But his wasn't. His wasn't at all.

* * *

Wiping her damp palms down the skirt of the horrible dress, Sophie stood in the middle of the portrait hall, halfway between the staircase and the closed doors to the drawing room. She was still shaking with horror and adrenaline and vile, unwelcome arousal and the urge to run back up to her bedroom, throw her things into her bag and slip quietly out of the servants' entrance was almost overwhelming. Wasn't that the way she'd always dealt with things—the way her mother had shown her? When the going got tough you walked away. You told yourself it didn't matter and you weren't bothered, and just to show you meant it you packed up and moved on.

The catering staff were putting the finishing touches to the buffet in the dining room, footsteps ringing on the flagstones as they brought up more champagne in ice buckets with which to greet the guests who would start arriving any minute. Sophie hesitated, biting down on her throbbing lip as for a moment she let herself imagine getting on a train and speeding through the darkness back to London, where she'd never have to see Kit Fitzroy again...

She felt a stab of pain beneath her ribs, but at that moment one of the enormous doors to the drawing room opened and Jasper appeared.

'Ah, there you are, angel! I thought you might have got lost again so I was just coming to see if I could find you.'

He started to come towards her, and Sophie saw his eyes sweep over her, widening along with his smile as he came closer.

'Saints Alive, Sophie Greenham, that *dress*...'

'I know,' Sophie croaked. 'Don't say it. It's dire.'

'It's not.' Slowly Jasper circled around her, looking her up and down as an incredulous expression spread across his face. 'How *could* we have got it so wrong? It might have been cheap as chips and looked like a shroud on the hanger, but on you it's bloody dynamite.' He gave a low whistle. 'Have you seen yourself? No red-blooded, straight male will be able to keep his hands off you.'

She gave a slightly hysterical laugh. 'Darling, don't you believe it.'

'Soph?' Jasper looked at her in concern. 'You OK?'

Oh, hell, what was she doing? She'd come here to shield him from the prejudices of his family, and so far she'd only succeeded in making things more awkward for him. The fact that his brother was the kind of cold-blooded, ruthless bastard who would stop at nothing to preserve the purity of the Fitzroy name and reputation was all the more reason she should give this her all.

'I'm fine.' Digging her nails into the palms of her hands, she raised her chin and smiled brightly. 'And you look gorgeous. There's something about a man in black tie that I find impossible to resist.'

Wasn't that the truth?

'Good.' Jasper pressed a fleeting kiss to her cheek and, taking hold of her hand, pulled her forwards. 'In that case, let's get this party started. Personally, I intend to get stuck into the champagne right now, before guests arrive and we have to share it.'

Head down, Kit walked quickly in the direction of the King's Hall—not because he was in any hurry to get there, but because he knew from long experience that looking purposeful was the best way to avoid getting trapped into conversation.

The last thing he felt like doing was talking to anyone.

As he went up the stairs the music got louder. Obviously keen to recapture his youthful prowess on the dance floor Ralph had hired a swing band, who were energetically working their way through the back catalogue of The Beatles. The strident tones of trumpet and saxophone swelled beneath the vaulted ceiling and reverberated off the walls.

Kit paused at the top of the flight of shallow steps into the huge space. The dance floor was a mass of swirling silks and velvets but even so his gaze was instantly drawn to the girl in the plain, narrow black dress in the midst of the throng. She was dancing with Ralph, Kit noticed, feeling himself tense inexplicably as he saw his father's large, practised hand splayed across the small of Sophie's back.

They suited each other very well, he thought with an inward sneer, watching the way the slit in Sophie's dress opened up as she danced to reveal a seductive glimpse of smooth, pale thigh. Ralph was a lifelong womaniser and philanderer, and Sophie Greenham seemed to be pretty indiscriminate in her favours, so there was no reason why she shouldn't make it a Fitzroy hat-trick. He turned away in disgust.

'Kit darling! I thought it must be you—not many people fill a dinner jacket that perfectly, though I must say I'm rather disappointed you're not in dress uniform tonight.'

Kit's heart sank as Sally Rothwell-Hyde grasped his shoulders and enveloped him in a cloud of asphyxiating perfume as she stretched up to kiss him on both cheeks. 'I saw the picture on the front of the paper, you dark horse,' she went on, giving him a girlish look from beneath spidery eyelashes. 'You looked utterly mouth-watering, and the medal did rather add to the heroic effect. I was hoping to see it on you.'

'Medals are only worn on uniform,' Kit remarked, trying to muster the energy to keep the impatience from his voice. 'And being in military dress uniform amongst this crowd would have had a slight fancy-dress air about it, don't you think?'

'Very dashing fancy dress, though, darling.' Leaning in close to make herself heard above the noise of the band, Sally fluttered her eyelashes, which were far too thick and lustrous to be anything but fake. 'Couldn't you have indulged us ladies?'

Kit's jaw clenched as he suppressed the urge to swear. To Sally Rothwell-Hyde and her circle of ladies who lunched, his uniform was just a prop from some clichéd fantasy, his medals were nothing more than covetable accessories. He doubted that it had crossed her mind for a moment what he had gone through to get them. The lost lives they represented.

His gaze moved over her sunbed-tanned shoulder as he looked for an escape route, but she wasn't finished with him yet. 'Such a shame about you and Alexia,' she pouted. 'Olympia said she was absolutely heartbroken, poor thing. She's taken Lexia skiing this weekend, to cheer her up. Perhaps she'll meet some hunky instructor and be swept off her skis…'

Kit understood that this comment was intended to make him wild with jealousy, but since it didn't he could think of nothing to say. Sophie was still dancing with Ralph, but more slowly now, both of his hands gripping her narrow waist while the band, ironically, played 'Can't Buy Me Love'. She had her back to Kit, so as she inclined her head to catch something his father said Kit could see the creamy skin at the nape of her neck and suddenly remembered the silky, sexy underwear that had spilled out of her broken bag yesterday. He wondered what she was wearing under that sober black dress.

'Is that her replacement?'

Sally's slightly acerbic voice cut into his thoughts, which was probably just as well. Standing beside him, she had followed the direction of his stare, and now took a swig of champagne and looked at him pointedly over the rim of her glass.

'No,' Kit replied shortly. 'That's Jasper's girlfriend.'

'Oh! *Really*?' Her ruthlessly plucked eyebrows shot up and she turned to look at Sophie again, murmuring, 'I must say I never really thought there was anything in those rumours.' Before Kit could ask her what the hell she meant her eyes had narrowed shrewdly. 'Who is she? She looks vaguely familiar from somewhere.'

'She's an actress. Maybe you've seen her in something.' His voice was perfectly steady, though his throat suddenly felt as if he'd swallowed gravel.

'An actress,' Sally repeated thoughtfully. 'Typical Jasper. So, what's she like?'

Lord, all that champagne and he didn't have a drink himself. Where the hell were the bloody waiters? Kit looked around as his mind raced, thinking of a suitable answer. *She's an unscrupulous liar and as shallow as a puddle, but on the upside she's the most alive person I've ever met and she kisses like an angel...*

'I'll get Jasper to introduce you,' he said blandly, moving away. 'You can see for yourself.'

Just as Sophie was beginning to suspect that the band were playing the Extended-Groundhog-Club-Remix version of 'Can't Buy Me Love' and that she would be locked for ever in Ralph Fitzroy's damp and rather-too-intimate clutches, the song came to a merciful end.

She'd been relieved when he'd asked her to dance as it had offered a welcome diversion from the task of Avoiding Kit, which had been the sole focus of her evening until then.

'Gosh—these shoes are murder to dance in!' she exclaimed brightly, stepping backwards and forcing Ralph to loosen his death-grip on her waist.

Ralph took a silk handkerchief from the top pocket of his dinner jacket and mopped his brow. Sophie felt a jolt of unease at the veins standing out in his forehead, the dark red flush in his cheeks, and suddenly wondered if it was lechery that had made him cling to her so tightly, or necessity. 'Darling girl, thank you for the dance,' he wheezed. 'You've made an old man very happy on his birthday. Look—here's Jasper to reclaim you.'

Slipping through the people on the dance floor, Jasper raised his hand in greeting. 'Sorry to break you two up, but I have people demanding to meet you, Soph. Pa, you don't mind if I snatch her away, do you?'

'Be my guest. I need a—' he broke off, swaying slightly, looking around '—need to—'

Sophie watched him weave slightly unsteadily through the crowd as Jasper grabbed her hand and started to pull her forwards. 'Jasper—your father,' she hissed, casting a worried glance over her shoulder. 'Is he OK? Maybe you should go with him?'

'He's fine,' Jasper said airily. 'This is the standard Hawksworth routine. He knocks back the booze, goes and sleeps it off for half an hour, then comes back stronger than ever and out-parties everyone else. Don't worry. A friend of my mother's is dying to meet you.'

He ran lightly up the steps and stopped in front of a petite woman in a strapless dress of aquamarine chiffon that showed off both her tan and the impressive diamonds around her crêpey throat. Her eyes were the colour of Bombay Sapphire gin and they swept over Sophie in swift appraisal as Jasper introduced her.

'Sophie, this is Sally Rothwell-Hyde, bridge partner-in-crime of my mother and all round bad influence. Sally—the girl of my dreams, Sophie—'

An icy wash of panic sluiced through her.

Great. Just *perfect*. She'd thought that there was no way that an evening that had started so disastrously could get any worse, but it seemed that fate had singled her out to be the victim of not one but several humiliating practical jokes. Just as Olympia Rothwell-Hyde used to do at school.

'Pleased to meet you,' Sophie cut in quickly before Jasper said her surname.

'Sophie…'

Sally Rothwell-Hyde's face bore a look of slight puzzlement as her eyes—so horribly reminiscent of the cold, china-doll blue of her daughter's—bored into Sophie. 'I'm trying to place you. Perhaps I know your parents?'

'I don't think so.'

Damn, she'd said that far too quickly. Sweat was prickling between her shoulder blades and gathering in the small of her back, and she felt slightly sick. She moistened her lips. Think of it as being onstage, she told herself desperately as the puzzled look was replaced by one of surprise and Sally Rothwell-Hyde gave a tinkling laugh.

'Gosh—well, if it isn't that I can't think what it could be.' Her eyes narrowed. 'You must be about the same age as my daughter. You're not a friend of Olympia's, are you?'

Breathe, Sophie told herself. She just had to imagine she was in the audience, watching herself playing the part, delivering the lines. It was a fail-safe way of coping with stage fright. Distance. Calm. Step outside yourself. Inhabit the character. And above all resist the urge to shriek, *A friend of that poisonous cow? Are you insane?'*

She arranged her face into a thoughtful expression. 'Olympia Rothwell-Hyde?' She said the loathed name hesitantly, as if hearing it for the first time, then shook her head, with just a hint of apology. 'It doesn't ring any bells. Sorry. Gosh, isn't it warm in here now? I'm absolutely dying of thirst after all that dancing, so if you'll excuse me I must just go and find a drink. Isn't it ironic to be surrounded by champagne when all you want is water?'

She began to move away before she finished speaking, glancing quickly at Jasper in a silent plea for him to rein back his inbred chivalry and keep quiet. He missed it entirely.

'I'll get—'

'No, darling, please. You stay and chat. I'll be back in a moment.'

She went down the steps again and wove her way quickly through the knots of people at the edge of the dance floor. Along the length of the hall there were sets of double doors out onto the castle walls and someone had opened one of them, letting in a sharp draft of night air. Sophie's footsteps stalled and she drank it in gratefully. It was silly—she'd spent the twenty-four hours since she'd arrived at Alnburgh freezing half to death and would have found it impossible to imagine being glad of the cold.

But then she'd have found it impossible to imagine a lot of the things that had happened in the last twenty-four hours.

A waiter carrying a tray laden with full glasses was making his way gingerly along the edge of the dance floor. He glanced apologetically at Sophie as she approached. 'Sorry, madam, I'm afraid this is sparkling water. If you'd like champagne I can—'

'Nope. Water's perfect. Thank you.' She took a glass, downed it in one and took another, hoping it might ease the throbbing in her head. At the top of the steps at the other end of the hall she could see Jasper still talking to Olympia Rothwell-Hyde's mother, so she turned and kept walking in the opposite direction.

She would explain to Jasper later. Right now the only thing on her mind was escape.

Stepping outside was like slipping into still, clear, icy water. The world was blue and white, lit by a paper-lantern moon hanging high over the beach. The quiet rushed in on her, as sudden and striking an assault on her senses as the breathtaking cold.

Going forwards to lean on the wall, she took in a gulp of air. It was so cold it flayed the inside of her lungs, and she let it go again in a cloud of white as she looked down. Far, far beneath her the rocks were sharp-edged and silvered by moonlight, and she found herself remembering Kit's voice as he told her about the desperate countess, throwing herself off the walls to her death. Down there? Sophie leaned further over, trying to imagine how things could have possibly been bleak enough for her to resort to such a brutal solution.

'It's a long way down.'

Sophie jumped so violently that the glass slipped from her hand and spiralled downwards in a shower of sparkling droplets. Her hand flew to her mouth, but not before she'd sworn, savagely and succinctly. In the small silence that followed she heard the sound of the glass shattering on the rocks below.

Kit Fitzroy came forwards slowly, so she could see the sardonic arch of his dark brows. 'Sorry. I didn't mean to startle you.'

Sophie gave a slightly wild laugh. 'Really? After what happened earlier, forgive me if I don't believe that for a second and just assume that's exactly what you meant to do, probably in the hope that it might result in another "accident" like the one that befell the last unsuitable woman to be brought home by a Fitzroy.'

She was talking too fast, and her heart was still banging against her ribs like a hammer on an anvil. She couldn't be sure it was still from the fright he'd just given her, though. Kit Fitzroy just seemed to have that effect on her.

'What a creative imagination you have.'

'Somehow it doesn't take too much creativity to imagine that you'd want to get rid of me.' She turned round, looking out across the beach again, to avoid having to look at him. 'You went to quite a lot of trouble to set me up and manipulate me earlier, after all.'

He came to stand beside her, resting his forearms on the top of the wall.

'It was no trouble. You were depressingly easy to manipulate.'

His voice was soft, almost intimate, and entirely at odds with the harshness of the words. But he was right, she acknowledged despairingly. She had been a pushover.

'You put me in an impossible position.'

'It wasn't impossible at all,' he said gravely. 'It would have been extremely workable, *if* I'd ever intended to let it get that far, which I didn't. Anyway, you're right. I do want to get rid of you, but since I'd have to draw the line at murder I'm hoping you'll leave quietly.'

'Leave?' Sophie echoed stupidly. A drumbeat of alarm had started up inside her head, in tandem with the dull throb from earlier. She hadn't seen this coming, and suddenly she didn't know what to say any more, how to play it. What had started off as being a bit of a game, a secret joke between her and Jasper, had spun out of control somewhere along the line.

'Yes. Leave Alnburgh.'

In contrast with the chaotic thoughts that were rushing through her brain, his voice was perfectly emotionless as he straightened up and turned to face her.

'I gather from Tatiana that Jasper's planning to stay on for a few days, but I think it would be best if you went back to London as soon as possible. The rail service on Sundays is minimal, but there's a train to Newcastle at about eleven in the morning and you can get a connection from there. I'll arrange for Jensen to give you a lift to the station.'

Sophie was glad she had the wall to lean on because she wasn't sure her legs would hold her up otherwise. She didn't turn to look at him, but was still aware of his height and the power contained in his lean body. It made her quail inside but it also sent a gush of hot, treacherous longing through her. She laughed awkwardly.

'Well, Major Fitzroy, you've got it all worked out, haven't you? And what about Jasper? Or have you forgotten him?'

'It's Jasper I'm thinking of.'

'Ah.' Sophie smacked herself comically on the forehead. 'Silly me, because I thought all this was for your benefit. I thought you wanted me gone because my face and my clothes and my accent don't fit and because I'm not scared of you like everyone else is. Oh, yes, and also because, no matter how much you'd like to pretend otherwise, you weren't entirely faking what happened earlier.'

For a second she wondered if she'd gone too far as some emotion she couldn't quite read flared in the icy fathoms of his eyes, but it was quickly extinguished.

'No.' His voice was ominously soft. 'I want you gone because you're dangerous.'

The anger that had fuelled her last outburst seemed suddenly to have run out. Now she felt tired and defeated, as the stags on the walls must have felt when the Fitzroy guns had appeared on the horizon.

'And what am I supposed to tell him?'

Kit shrugged. 'You'll think of something, I'm sure. Your remarkable talent for deception should make it easy for you to find a way to let him down gently. Then he can find someone who'll treat him with the respect he deserves.'

'Someone who also fits your narrow definition of suitable.' Sophie gave a painful smile, thinking of Sergio. The irony would have been funny if it hadn't all got so serious, and so horribly humiliating. 'Gosh,' she went on, 'who would have guessed that under that controlling, joyless exterior beat such a romantic heart?'

'I'm not romantic.' Kit turned towards her again, leaning one hip against the wall as he fixed her with his lazy, speculative gaze. 'I just have this peculiar aversion to unscrupulous social climbers. As things stand at the moment I'm prepared

to accept that you're just a pretty girl with issues around commitment and the word "no", but if you stay I'll be forced to
take a less charitable view.'

From inside came a sudden chorus of 'Happy Birthday to
You.' Automatically Sophie looked through the window to
where everyone had assembled to watch Ralph cut his birthday cake. The light from the huge chandeliers fell on the
perma-tanned backs of the women in their evening dresses
and made the diamonds at their throats glitter, while amongst
them the dinner-suited men could have been the rich and the
privileged from any era in the last hundred years.

I really, really do not belong here, Sophie thought.

Part of her wanted to stand up to Kit Fitzroy and challenge
his casual, cruel assumptions about her, as her mother would
have done, but she knew from bitter experience that there was
no point. Inside, through the press of people, she could see
Sally Rothwell-Hyde, all gleaming hair and expensive white
teeth, as she sang, and suddenly Sophie was sixteen again,
standing in the corridor at school with her packed trunk and
her hockey stick beside her, watching through the glass doors
of the hall as the other girls sang the school hymn and she
waited for Aunt Janet to arrive.

She clenched her teeth together to stop them chattering,
suddenly realising that she was frozen to the bone. Inside the
rousing chorus of 'Happy Birthday' was coming to an end. If
she went in now she could probably slip past unnoticed and
reach the staircase while all eyes were focused on the cake.

Lifting her chin, she met Kit Fitzroy's eyes. They were as
cold and silvery as the surface of the moonlit sea.

'OK. You win. I'll go.' She faked a smile. 'But do me a favour—spend some time with Jasper when I'm gone, would
you? You'll like him when you get to know him.'

She didn't wait for his reply. Turning on her heel, holding
herself very upright, she walked back to the door and pulled

it open, stepping into the warmth just as the party-goers finished singing and burst into a noisy round of cheering and ap-
plause. Sophie paused as her eyes adjusted to the brightness
in the hall. At the top of the steps at the far end an elaborate
cake made to look like Alnburgh Castle stood on a damask-
covered table, the light from the candles glowing in its battlements briefly illuminating Ralph's face as he leaned forwards
to blow them out.

He seemed to hesitate for a moment, his mouth opening in
an O of surprise. And then he was pitching sideways, grasping the tablecloth and pulling it, and the cake, with him as
he fell to the floor.

CHAPTER EIGHT

'SOMEBODY *do* something!'

Tatiana's voice, shrill with panic, echoed through the sudden silence. Before Sophie had time to process what had happened Kit was pushing past her, shrugging his jacket off as he ran across the hall towards the figure on the floor. The stunned onlookers parted to let him through, recognising by some mutual instinct that he was the person to deal with this shocking turn of events. As the crowd shifted and fell back Sophie caught a glimpse of Ralph's face. It was the colour of old parchment.

Kit dropped to his knees beside his father, undoing his silk bow tie with swift, deft fingers and working loose the button at his throat.

'Does anyone know how to do mouth-to-mouth or CPR?' he shouted.

The tense silence was broken only by the shuffling of feet as people looked around hopefully, but no one spoke. Before she could think through the wisdom of what she was doing Sophie found herself moving forwards.

'I do.'

Kit didn't speak or look up as she knelt down opposite him. Bunching up his dinner jacket, he put it beneath Ralph's feet.

'Is he breathing?' she asked in a low voice.

'No.'

Tatiana, supported now on each side by male guests, let out a wail of distress.

'Jasper,' Kit barked icily, 'take her to the drawing room. You can phone for an ambulance from there. Tell them the roads are bad and they'll need to send a helicopter. Do it *now*.'

Bastard, thought Sophie in anguish, glancing round to where Jasper was standing, his face ashen against his black dinner jacket, his eyes wide and glassy with shock. How dared Kit talk to him like that at a time like this? But his voice seemed to snap Jasper out of his trance of shock and he gathered himself, doing as he was told.

'Breathing or heart?'

He was talking to her, Sophie realised. 'Breathing,' she said quickly, and regretted it almost straight away. At the moment she could barely breathe for herself, never mind for Ralph too, but there was no time for second thoughts.

Kit had already pulled his father's shirt open and started chest compressions, his lips moving silently as he counted. Sophie's hand shook as she tilted Ralph's head back and held his jaw. His skin had a clammy chill to it that filled her with dread, but also banished any lingering uncertainty.

OK, so she'd only done this on fellow actors in a TV hospital drama, but she'd been taught the technique by the show's qualified medical advisor and right now that looked like Ralph's best hope. She had to do it. And fast.

Kit's hands stilled. 'Ready?'

For the briefest second their eyes met, and she felt an electrical current crackle through her, giving her strength. She took in a breath and bent her head, placing her mouth over Ralph's and exhaling slowly.

The seconds ticked by, measured only by the steady tide of her breath, the rhythmic movement of Kit's hands. They took it in turns, each acutely aware of the movements of the other. It was like a dance in which she let Kit lead her, watching him for cues, her eyes fixed unwaveringly on his as she waited for his signal. Fifteen rapid compressions. Two long, slow breaths.

And then wait.

Sophie lost track of time. She lost track of everything except Kit's eyes, his strong, tanned hands locked together on Ralph's grey chest...the stillness of that chest. Sometimes she thought there were signs of life—too tenuous for her to feel relief, too strong for her to give up, so again and again she bent her head and breathed for Ralph, willing the life and heat and adrenaline of her own body into the inert figure on the floor.

And then at last as she lifted her head she saw Ralph's chest convulse in a sharp, gasping breath of his own. Her gaze flew to Kit's face as he looked down at his father, pressing his fingers to Ralph's neck, waiting to see if a pulse had returned. Except for the small frown of concentration between his brows it was expressionless, but a muscle twitched in his jaw.

And then Ralph breathed again and Kit looked at her.

'Good girl.'

The sound of running feet echoed through the hall, breaking the spell. Sophie's head jerked round and she was surprised to see that the guests had all vanished and the huge room was empty now—except for the helicopter paramedics coming towards them, like orange-suited angels from some sci-fi film.

Kit got to his feet in one lithe movement and dragged a hand through his hair. For the first time Sophie saw that he was grey with exhaustion beneath his tan.

'He's been unconscious for about seventeen minutes. He's breathing again. Pulse is weak but present.'

A female paramedic carrying a defibrillator kit glanced at him, then did a classic double take. 'Well done,' she said in a tone that bordered on awestruck. 'That makes our job so much easier.'

'Come on, sweetheart. We can take over now.'

Sophie jumped. One of the other paramedics was kneeling beside her, gently edging her out of the way as he fitted an oxygen mask over Ralph's face.

'Oh, I'm so sorry,' she muttered, attempting to get to her feet. 'I was miles away...I mean, I wasn't thinking...'

Her dress was too tight and her legs were numb from kneeling, making it difficult to stand. Somehow Kit was beside her, his hand gripping her elbow as she swayed on her high heels.

'OK?'

She nodded, suddenly unable to speak for the lump of emotion that had lodged in her throat. Relief, perhaps. Delayed shock. Powerful things that made her want to collapse into his arms and sob like a little girl.

She had no idea why. Even when she was a little girl she couldn't ever remember sobbing so now was hardly the time to start. And Kit Fitzroy, who not half an hour ago had coldly ordered her to leave his family home, was definitely not the person to start on.

Raising her chin and swallowing hard, she stepped away from him, just as Jasper appeared.

'Soph—what's h—?'

He stopped, his reddened eyes widening in horror as the paramedics strapped his father's body onto the stretcher. Quickly Sophie went to his side, putting her arms around his trembling body.

'It's OK,' she soothed, suddenly poleaxed with exhaustion. 'He's alive, he's breathing and he's in the very best hands now.'

Briefly he leaned against her and she smelled the booze on his breath and felt his shoulders shake as he sobbed. 'Sophie, thank God you were here.' He pulled away, hastily wiping his eyes. 'I should go. To the hospital, to be with Mum.'

Sophie nodded.

'I'm afraid there's only room for one person in the helicopter,' the pretty blonde paramedic apologised as they lifted the stretcher. 'The rest of the family will have to follow by car.'

Momentary panic flashed across Jasper's face as he made a mental calculation of alcohol units.

'I can't—'

'I can.' Kit stepped forwards. 'Tatiana can go in the helicopter and I'll take Jasper.' His eyes met Sophie's. 'Are you coming?'

For a long moment they looked at each other. Blood beat in Sophie's ears and her heart seemed to swell up, squeezing the air from her lungs. She shook her head.

'No. No, I'll stay and make sure everything's OK here.'

For a few minutes—seventeen apparently, who knew?—they had shared something. A connection. But it was gone again now. She might just have helped to save his father's life, but that didn't alter the fact that Kit Fitzroy had made it very clear he wanted her out of Jasper's. And his. The sooner the better.

Hours later, standing in the softly lit corridor of the private hospital, Kit rubbed a hand over his stinging eyes.

He could defuse a landmine and dismantle the most complex and dangerous IED in extreme heat and under enemy fire, but he couldn't for the life of him work out how to get a cup of instant coffee from the machine in front of him.

Stabilised by drugs and hooked up to bags of fluid, Ralph was sleeping peacefully now. The hospital staff, hearing that Lord Hawksworth was on his way, had telephoned Ralph's private physician at home. He had arranged for Ralph to be admitted to the excellently equipped private hospital in

Newcastle, which looked like a hotel and had facilities for relatives to stay too. Once she was reassured that her husband wasn't in any immediate danger Tatiana, claiming exhaustion, had accepted the sleeping pill the nurse offered and retired to the room adjoining Ralph's. Jasper, who had obviously knocked back enough champagne to float half the British Navy, didn't need medication to help him sleep and was now snoring softly in the chair beside Ralph's bed.

Which just left Kit.

He was used to being awake when everyone else was asleep. The silence and stillness of the small hours of the morning were tediously familiar to him, but he had found that the only way of coping with insomnia was to accept it. To relax, even if sleep itself was elusive.

He groaned inwardly. Tonight even that was out of the question.

Back in Ralph's room a small light was on over the bed, by which Kit could see his father's skin had lost its bluish tinge. An image floated in front of his eyes of Sophie, lowering her head, her mouth opening to fill Ralph's lungs with oxygen, again and again.

He closed his eyes momentarily. Details he'd been too focused to take in at the time rising to the surface of his mind. The bumps of her spine standing out beneath the pale skin at the base of her neck. Her green gaze fixing on his in a way that shut out the rest of the world. In a way that showed that she trusted him.

He winced. In view of everything that had taken place between them that evening, that was something of a surprise.

But then there was quite a lot about Sophie Greenham that surprised him, such as her ability to make a cheap dress look like something from a Bond Street boutique. The way she'd stood up to him. Fought back. The fact that she could give the kiss of life well enough to make a dead man breathe again.

And another one feel again.

Rotating his aching shoulders, he paced restlessly over to the window, willing away the throb of arousal that had instantly started up inside him again.

The incident in the wine cellar seemed like days rather than hours ago, and thinking about it now he felt a wave of self-disgust. He had told himself he was acting in Jasper's best interests, that somehow he was deliberately seducing his brother's girlfriend *for his benefit.*

Locking his fingers behind his neck, Kit exhaled deeply and made himself confront the unwelcome truth Sophie had flung at him earlier. He had done it to prove himself right, to get some small, petty revenge on his father and score a private victory over the girl who had so unsettled him from the moment he'd first laid eyes on her. He had barely thought of Jasper at all.

But he forced himself to look at him now. Slumped in the chair, Jasper slept on, his cheek resting on one hand, his closed eyelids red and puffy from crying. He looked very young and absurdly fragile.

A pickaxe of guilt smashed through Kit's head.

Always look out for your weakest man—his army training overruled the natural inclination forged by his family circumstances. *Never exploit that weakness, or take risks with it.* Even when it had irritated the hell out of you for as long as you could remember.

Jasper might lack the steel Kit was used to in the men he served with, but that didn't give Kit the right to kiss his girlfriend, just to show that he could. And to enjoy kissing her, so much that he had spent the evening thinking of nothing else but kissing her again. Right up until the moment he'd ordered her to leave.

Horrified realisation jolted through him. He swore sharply.

'Are you OK there?'

Kit spun round.

A plump, homely-looking nurse had appeared on silent feet and was checking the bag of fluid that was dripping into Ralph's arm. She glanced at Kit.

'Can I get you anything—coffee perhaps?'

'No, thanks.' Picking up his car keys, he headed for the door, his need for caffeine paling into insignificance in the light of this new imperative. To get back to Alnburgh and make sure that Sophie Greenham was still there. And that she would stay. For as long as Jasper needed her.

The red tail lights of the last catering van had disappeared under the archway and the sound of the engines faded into a thick silence that was broken only by the distant hiss of the sea. Shivering with cold and fear, Sophie turned and went back inside, shutting the massive oak door with a creaking sound that came straight from *The Crypt* and sliding the bolts across with clumsy, frozen fingers.

She still felt weak with shock and there was a part of her that wished she were in one of those vans, sweeping down the drive to civilisation and a warm bed in a centrally heated home. Going through the hallway beneath the rows of glassy eyes, she hummed the opening lines of 'My Favourite Things', but if anything the eerie echo of her voice through the empty rooms made her feel more freaked out than ever. She shut up again.

Her mind would insist on replaying events from the moment she'd seen Ralph fall, like one of those annoying TV adverts that seemed to be on twice in every break. She found herself hanging on to the memory of Kit's strength and assurance, his control of the situation. And the way, when her resolve was faltering, he'd wrapped her in his gaze and said 'good girl'.

Good girl.

He'd also said an awful lot of other things to her tonight, she reminded herself with a sniff, so it was completely illogical that those two should have made such an impression. But he was the kind of stern, upright person from whom you couldn't help but crave approval, that was why it was such a big deal. And that was the biggest irony of all. Because he was also the kind of person who would never in a million years approve of someone like her.

Miserably she switched the lights out and went into the portrait hall.

Not just the person he thought she was—Jasper's two-timing girlfriend—but the real Sophie Greenham, the girl who had been haphazardly brought up on a bus, surrounded by an assortment of hippies and dropouts. The girl who had no qualifications, and who'd blown her chance to get any by being expelled from school. The girl whose family tree didn't even stretch back as far as her own father, and whose surname came—not from William the Conqueror—but from the peace camp where her mother had discovered feminism, cannabis and self-empowerment.

In her gilded frame opposite the staircase the superior expression on Tatiana's painted face said it all.

Sophie flicked off the light above the portrait and trailed disconsolately into the King's Hall. The chandeliers still blazed extravagantly, but it was like looking at an empty stage after the play had finished and the actors had gone home. She had to steel herself to look at the place where Ralph had collapsed, but the caterers had cleaned up so that no evidence remained of the drama that had taken place there only a few hours earlier. She was just switching the lights off when she noticed something lying on the steps. Her pulse quickened a little as she went over to pick it up.

Kit's jacket.

She stood for a second, biting her lip as she held it. It *was* very cold, and there was absolutely no way she was going to go upstairs along all those dark passageways where the countess's ghost walked to get a jumper. Quickly she closed her eyes and slid it across her shoulders. Pulling it close around her, she breathed in the scent of him and revelled in the memory of his kiss...

A kiss that should never have happened, she told herself crossly, opening her eyes. A kiss that in the entire history of disastrous, mistaken, ill-advised kisses would undoubtedly make the top ten. She had to stop this sudden, stupid crush in its tracks; it was doomed from the outset, which of course was why it felt so powerful. Didn't she always want what she knew would never be hers?

In the drawing room the fire had burned down to ashes. There was no way she was going to brave the ice-breathed darkness upstairs, so she piled logs on, hoping there was enough heat left for them to catch.

In the meantime she would keep the jacket on, though...

It was going to be a long, cold night.

Perched on its platform of rock above the sea, Alnburgh Castle was visible for ten miles away on the coast road, so by the time Kit pulled into the courtyard he already knew that it was entirely in darkness.

Lowering his head against the sabre-toothed wind, he let himself in through the kitchen door, remembering how he'd often done the same thing when he came home from boarding school for the holidays and found the place deserted because Ralph and Tatiana were at a party, or had gone away.

He'd never been particularly bothered to find the castle empty back then, but now…

Lord, she'd better still be here.

His footsteps sounded as loud as gunshots as he walked through the silent rooms. Passing the foot of the stairs, he glanced at the grandfather clock and felt a sudden beat of hope. It was half past three in the morning—of course—she'd be in bed, wouldn't she?

He took the stairs two at a time, aware that his heart was beating hard and unevenly. Outside the door to her room he tipped his head back and inhaled deeply, clenching his hand into a fist and holding it there for a second before knocking very softly. There was no answer, so, hardly breathing, he opened the door.

It was immediately obvious the room was empty. The curtains were undrawn, the moonlight falling on a neatly made bed, an uncluttered chest of drawers.

She might be in bed, he thought savagely. The question was, whose?

Adrenaline was circulating like neat alcohol through his bloodstream as he went back down the stairs. How the hell was he going to break the news to Jasper that she'd gone?

And that it was all his fault?

He headed for the drawing room, suddenly in desperate need of a drink. Pushing open the door, he was surprised to see that the fire was hissing softly in the grate, spilling out a halo of rosy light into the empty room. He strode over to the table where the drinks tray was and was just about to turn on the light beside it when he stopped dead.

Sophie was lying on the rug in front of the fire, hidden from view by the sofa when he'd first come into the room. Her head was resting on one outstretched arm, and she'd pulled the pins from her hair so that it fell, gleaming, over the white skin of her wrist like a pool of warm, spilled syrup. She was lying on her side, wearing a man's dinner jacket, but even though it was miles too big for her it couldn't quite disguise the swooping contours of her hip and waist.

He let out a long, slow breath, unaware until that moment that he'd been holding it in. Tearing his gaze away from her with physical effort, he reached for a glass and splashed a couple of inches of brandy into it, then walked slowly around the sofa to stand over her.

If the impact of seeing her from behind had made him forget to breathe, the front view was even more disturbing. Her face was flushed from the warmth, and the firelight made exaggerated shadows beneath the dark lashes fanning over her cheeks and the hollow above the cupid's bow of her top lip. Tilting his head, he let his eyes move over her, inch by inch, adjusting his jaded perception of her to fit the firelit vision before him.

She looked...

He took a swallow of brandy, hoping it might wash away some of the less noble adjectives that arrived in his head, courtesy of six months spent in the company of a regiment of sex-starved men. *Vulnerable*, that was it, he thought with a pang. He remembered watching her sleep on the train and being struck by her self-containment. He frowned. Looking at her now, it appeared to him more like self-protection, as if she had retreated into some private space where she was safe and untouchable.

He felt a sudden jolt pass through him, like a tiny electric shock, and realised that her eyes had opened and she was looking up at him. Like a cat she raised herself into a sitting position, flexing the arm she'd been sleeping on, arching her spine.

'You're back,' she said in a voice that was breathy with sleep.

He took another mouthful of brandy, registering for the

first time the sheer relief he'd felt when he saw her, which had got rather subsumed by other, more urgent sensations.

'I thought you'd gone.'

It was as if he'd dropped an ice cube down her back. Getting to her feet, she turned away from him, smoothing the wrinkled dress down over her hips. He could see now that jacket she was wearing was his, and a fresh pulse of desire went through him.

'Sorry. Obviously I would have, but I didn't think there would be any trains in the middle of the night.' There was a slight hint of sarcasm in her voice, but it was a pale echo of her earlier bravado. 'And I didn't want to leave until I knew how Ralph was. Is he—?'

'He's the same. Stable.'

'Oh.' She turned to him then, her face full of tentative hope in the firelight. 'That's good, isn't it?'

Kit exhaled heavily, remembering the quiet determination with which she'd kept fighting to keep Ralph alive, reluctant to take the hope away. 'I don't know. It might be.'

'Oh.' She nodded once, quickly, and he knew she understood. 'How's Tatiana? And Jasper?'

'Both asleep when I left. They gave Tatiana a sleeping pill.' He couldn't keep the cynicism from his tone. 'Unsurprisingly Jasper didn't need one.'

Sophie's laugh had a break in it. 'Oh, God. He'll be unconscious until mid-morning. I hope the nurses have a megaphone and a bucket of iced water.'

Kit didn't smile. He came towards the sofa and leaned against the arm, swilling the last mouthful of brandy around his glass so that it glinted like molten sunlight. Warily, Sophie watched him, hardly able to breathe. The fire held both of them in an intimate circle, sealed together against the darkness of the room, the castle, the frozen world beyond.

'He was very emotional. I know he's had a lot to drink, but even so...'

Sophie sat down on the edge of a velvet armchair. 'That's Jasper. He can't help it. He wears his heart on his sleeve. It's one of the things I love most about him.'

'It's one of the things that irritate me most about him,' Kit said tersely. 'He was in bits all the way to the hospital—sobbing like a baby and saying over and over again that there was so much he still needed to say.'

Bloody hell, Jasper, Sophie thought desperately. Coming out to his family was one thing. Getting drunk and dropping heavy hints so they guessed enough to ask her was quite another. 'He was upset, that's all,' she said quickly, unable to keep the defensiveness from her tone. 'There's nothing wrong with showing emotion—some people might regard it as being normal, in fact. He'd just seen his father collapse in front of him and stop breathing—'

'Even so. This is just the beginning. If he can't cope now—'

'What do you mean, this is just the beginning?'

Kit got up and went to stand in front of the fire, looking into the flames. 'Who knows how long this will go on for? The doctors are saying he's stable, which Tatiana and Jasper seem to think is just a stage on the way back to complete recovery.'

'And you think differently,' Sophie croaked. Oh, dear. Something about the sight of his wide shoulders silhouetted against the firelight had made it hard to speak. She tucked her legs up beneath her, her whole body tightening around the fizz of arousal at its core.

'He was without oxygen for a long time,' Kit said flatly.

'Oh.' Sophie felt the air rush from her lungs and felt powerless to take in any more to replace it. She had tried. She had tried so hard, but it hadn't been enough.

'So what are you saying?'

'I'm saying it's highly likely he won't come out of this. That at some point in the next few days Jasper's going to have to deal with Ralph's death.'

'Oh. I see,' she said faintly. 'That soon?' Something about the way he was talking set alarm bells off in some distant part of her brain. He's going to tell me he wants me to leave now, she thought in panic. Tonight, before Jasper gets back...

'I think so.' His voice was low and emotionless. 'And if I'm right, I think it would be better if he didn't also have to deal with the girl he's crazy about running out on him.'

Steeling herself as if against a blow, Sophie blinked in confusion. 'But...I don't understand. You asked me to go...'

Kit turned around to look at her. The firelight gilded his cheekbones and brought an artificial warmth to his cold silver eyes. 'Things have changed,' he drawled softly, giving her an ironic smile. 'And now I'm asking you to stay. You've played the part of Jasper's doting girlfriend for two days. I'm afraid you'll just have to play it a bit longer.'

CHAPTER NINE

Kit was used to action. He was used to giving an order and having it obeyed, working out what needed to be done and doing it, and in the days that followed trying to penetrate the dense forest of bureaucracy that choked the Alnburgh estate tested his patience to the limit.

He spent most of his time in the library, which was one of the few staterooms at Alnburgh to have escaped the attention of Tatiana's interior designer. A huge oriel window overlooked the beach, and on a day like today, when sea, sky and sand were a Rothko study of greys, the bleakness of the view made the inside seem warm by comparison.

Putting the phone down after yet another frustrating conversation with the Inland Revenue, Kit glanced along the beach, subconsciously looking for the slender figure, bright hair whipped by the wind, who had made it so bloody difficult to concentrate yesterday. But apart from a couple of dog walkers the long crescent of sand was deserted.

He turned away, irritation mixing with relief.

It had been three days since Ralph's heart attack, three days since he'd asked Sophie to stay on at Alnburgh, and things had settled into a routine of sorts. Every morning he drove a pale, shaken Jasper and a tight-lipped Tatiana to the hospital in Newcastle to sit at Ralph's bedside, though Ralph remained unconscious and unaware of their vigil. He stayed long enough to have a brief consultation with one of the team of medical staff and then returned to Alnburgh to avoid Sophie and begin to work his way through the landslide of overdue bills, complaints from estate tenants and un-followed-up quotes from builders and surveyors about the urgent work the castle required.

It was a futile task, of that he was certain. Often, as he came across yet another invoice from Ralph's wine merchant or Tatiana's interior designer, he remembered Ralph saying, *I have every intention of lasting a lot more than seven years.*

Now it looked as if he wouldn't make it to seven days, and his inexplicable refusal to acknowledge the existence of British inheritance tax probably meant that the Alnburgh estate was doomed. It would be sold off in lots and the cas-tle would be turned into a hotel, or one of those awful con-ference centres where businessmen came for team-building weekends and bonding exercises.

Ironically, because in thirty-four years there Kit hadn't formed any kind of bond with the rest of his family.

He walked back to the desk, leaning on it for a moment with his arms braced and his head lowered, refusing to yield to the avalanche of anger and bitterness and sheer bloody frustration that threatened to bury him.

There's nothing wrong with showing emotion—some peo-ple might regard it as being normal.

Sophie's voice drifted through his head, and he straight-ened up, letting out a long, ragged breath. It was something that had happened with ridiculous regularity these last few days, when time and time again he'd found himself replay-ing conversations he'd had with her, thinking about things she'd said, and wondering what she'd say about other stuff.

It made him uncomfortable to suspect that a lot of the time she'd talked a lot of sense. He'd wanted to write her off as a lightweight. An airhead actress who was easy on the eye, and in other respects too, but who wasn't big on insight.

But if that was the case, why did he find himself wanting to talk to her so badly now?

Because Jasper was either drunk or hungover and Tatiana was—well, Tatiana, he thought wearily. Sophie was the only other person who hadn't lost the plot.

An outsider, just like him.

Sophie dreamed that she was being pulled apart by rough hands. She curled up tightly into a ball, hugging her knees to her chest, trying to stop shivering, trying to stop the hurting deep inside and calling out to Kit because he was the only one who could help her. She needed his strong, big hands to press down and stop the blood from coming.

She awoke to see a thin light breaking through the gap in the curtains. Her body was stiff with cold, and from the cramped position that she'd slept in, but as she unfurled her legs she felt a familiar spasm of pain in her stomach and let out a groan of dismay.

Her mind spooled backwards. Had it really been a month since that December night in Paris? Jean-Claude had called at the apartment in the early hours, reeking of wine and sweat and cigarettes, almost combusting with lust after an evening working on 'Nude with Lilies'. Bent double with period pain, Sophie had only gone down to let him in because she'd known he'd wake the whole street if she didn't. That might have been preferable to the unpleasant little scene that had followed. Jean-Claude had been unwilling to take no for an answer, and it was only thanks to the amount of booze he'd sunk that Sophie had been able to fend him off. He'd fallen asleep, snoring at ear-splitting volume, sprawled across the bed, and Sophie had spent the rest of the night sitting on a hard kitchen chair, curled around a hot-water bottle, deliberately not thinking of anything but the pain blossoming inside her.

Tentatively she sat up now, wincing as the fist in her belly tightened and twisted. Since she was thirteen she'd suffered seven kinds of hell every month with her period. The cramps always came first, but it wouldn't be long before the bleeding started. Which meant she'd better get herself to a chemist pretty quickly, since she hadn't come prepared and neither Tatiana nor Mrs Daniels were the kind of cosy, down-to-earth women she could ask for help. Just the thought of saying the words 'sanitary protection' to either of them brought her out in a cold sweat.

She got out of bed, stooping slightly with the pain, and reached for her clothes.

It was the coldest winter in forty years. The temperature in the castle hardly seemed to struggle above freezing, and Sophie was forced to abandon all ambitions of style in favour of the more immediate need to ward off death by hypothermia. This had meant plundering Jasper's wardrobe to supplement her own, and she'd taken to sleeping in his old school rugby shirt, which was made to keep out the chill of a games field in the depths of winter and was therefore just about suitable for the bedrooms at Alnburgh. She couldn't bear the thought of exposing any flesh to the icy air so pulled her jeans on with it, zipping them up with difficulty over her tender, swollen stomach, and grabbed her purse.

Going down the stairs, clutching the banister for support, she glanced at the grandfather clock in the hall below. Knickers, she'd slept late—Jasper would have gone to the hospital ages ago.

She felt a twist of anguish as she wondered if he'd been hungover again this morning. Sergio had been putting pressure on Jasper to let him come up and be with him through all this, and Jasper was finding it increasingly hard to deal with his divided loyalties. Sophie didn't blame him for trying, though. Kit had given her a hard enough time—what would he do to flamboyant, eccentric drama-queen Sergio?

Not kiss him, presumably…

'Morning. Just about.'

Talk of the devil. His sardonic, mocking voice startled her. That was why her mouth was suddenly dry and her heart had sped up ridiculously.

'Morning.'

She attempted to sound aloof and distracted, but as she hadn't spoken a word since she'd woken up she just sounded bad-tempered. He was wearing a dark blue cashmere sweater and in the defeated grey light of the bitter morning he looked tanned and incongruously handsome, like some modern-day heart-throb superimposed on a black and white background. Maybe that accounted for the bad-tempered tone slightly as well.

His deadpan gaze swept over her, one arched brow rising. 'Off to rugby training?'

She was confused for a second, until she remembered she was wearing Jasper's rugby shirt.

She faked an airy smile. 'I thought I'd give it a miss today and have a cigarette behind the bike sheds instead. To be honest, I'm not sure it's really my game.'

'Oh, I don't know,' he drawled quietly with the faintest smile. 'I think you'd make a pretty good hooker.'

'Very funny.' She kept going, forcing herself to hold herself more upright in spite of the feeling of having been kicked in the stomach by a horse. 'I'm going to the village shop. I need to pick up a few things.'

'Things?'

Bloody hell, why did she always feel the need to explain herself to him? If she hadn't said anything she wouldn't have put herself in the position of having to lie. Again.

'I'm coming down with a cold. Tissues, aspirin—that sort of thing.'

'I'm sure Mrs Daniels would be able to help you out with all that,' he said blandly. 'Would you like me to ask her?'

'No, thank you,' she snapped. The kicked-by-a-horse feeling was getting harder to ignore. She paused on the bottom step, clinging to the newel post as nausea rose inside her. The pain used to make her sick when she was younger and, though it hadn't happened for a few years, her body seemed to have developed a keen sense of comedy timing whenever Kit Fitzroy was around. 'I'll go myself, if that's OK? I wasn't aware I was under house arrest?'

From where she was standing his hooded eyes were on a level with hers. 'You're not.'

Sophie gave a brittle little laugh. 'Then why are you treating me like a criminal?'

He waited a moment before replying, looking at her steadily with those cold, opaque eyes. A muscle was flickering slightly in his taut, tanned cheek. 'I suppose,' he said with sinister softness, 'because I find it hard to believe that you've suddenly been struck with an urgent desire to go shopping when it's minus five outside and you're only half dressed.'

'I don't have time for this,' she muttered, going to move past him, desperate to escape the scrutiny of his gaze. Desperate for fresh air, even if it was of the Siberian variety. 'I'm dressed perfectly adequately.'

'I suppose it depends what for,' he said gravely as she passed him. 'Since you're clearly not wearing a bra.'

With a little gasp of outrage, Sophie looked down and saw that the neck of the rugby shirt was open wide enough to reveal a deep ravine of cleavage. Jasper's fourteen-year-old chest was obviously considerably smaller than hers. She snatched the collar and wrenched it together.

'Because I've just got out of bed.'

'And you're just about to rush into someone else's while Jasper's not here?' Kit suggested acidly.

That did it. The contempt in his voice, combined with another wringing cramp, made her lose her temper. 'No,' she cried, hands clenched into fists at her sides, cheeks flaming. 'I really *am* rushing to the village shop. In minus five temperatures and with stomach cramps that possibly register on the Richter scale, not because I *want* to, but because I'm about to start the period from hell and I am completely unprepared for it. So now perhaps you'll just let me go before it all gets messy.'

For a moment there was silence. Complete. Total. Kit took a step backwards, out of the orbit of her anger, and Sophie saw the spark of surprise in his eyes. And then the shutters went down and he was back in control.

'In that case you're not going anywhere,' he said with a faint, ironic smile. 'Or only as far as the library anyway—at least you won't freeze to death in there. Leave it to me. I'll be back as soon as I can.'

Sitting in the car and waiting for the fan to thaw the ice on the windscreen, Kit dropped his head into his hands.

He had always thought of himself as level-headed. Rational. Fair. A man who was ruled by sense rather than feeling. So in that encounter how come he'd emerged as some kind of bullying jailer?

Because there was something about this girl that made him lose reason. Something about her smile and her eyes and the way she tried to look haughty but could never quite pull it off that made him *feel* far too much. And still want to feel more.

Her body, for a start. All of it. Without clothes.

He started the engine with an unnecessary roar and shot forwards in a screech of tyres. Lord, no matter how incredible he found it, she was his younger brother's girlfriend and the only reason she was still here was because he'd ordered her to stay. That made two good reasons why he should be civil to her, so he'd better start by behaving less like a fascist dictator and more like a decent human being.

After that he could have a look through his address book and find someone who would be happy to supply him with the sexual release he so obviously needed before going back to his unit and channelling his energy into the blessedly absorbing task of staying alive.

Sophie managed to wait until Kit had left the library and shut the door before putting her hands over her burning cheeks and letting out a low moan of mortification.

Saints in heaven, why had she blurted all that out? She was supposed to be an *actress*. Why couldn't she ever manage to act mysterious, or poised, or *elegant*?

Especially around Kit Fitzroy, who must be used to silken officer's-wife types, with perfect hair and manners to match. Women who would never do anything as vulgar as swear or menstruate. Or lose their temper. Or kiss someone without realising they were being set up, or put themselves in a position where someone would want to set them up in the first place...

Women with class, in other words.

She let her hands drop again and looked up, noticing the room properly for the first time. Even seen through a fog of humiliation she could see straight away that it was different from the other rooms she'd been in at Alnburgh. There was none of the blowsy ostentation of the drawing room with its raw-silk swagged curtains and designer wallpaper, nor the comfortless, neglected air of upstairs. In here everything was faded, used and cherished, from the desk piled with papers

in the window to the enormous velvet Knole sofa in front
of the fire.

But it was the books that jolted her out of her self-pity.
Thousands of them, in shelves stretching up to the high ceiling, with a narrow galleried walkway halfway up. Where she
had grown up the only books were the few tattered self-help
manuals that the women at the peace camp had circulated between themselves, with titles like *Freeing the Warrior Woman
Within* and *The Harmonious Vegan*, and even when Sophie
had managed to get hold of a book of her own from a second
hand shop or jumble sale there had never been anywhere quiet
to read it. She had always dreamed of a room like this.

Almost reverentially she walked along the bookcases, trailing her finger along the spines of the books. They were mostly
old, faded to a uniform brown, the gold titles almost unread-
able, but in the last section, by the window, there were some
more modern paperbacks—Dick Francis, Agatha Christie
and—joy—a handful of Georgette Heyer. Moving the faded
curtain aside, Sophie gave a little squeak of delight as she
spotted *Devil's Cub*, and felt a new respect for Tatiana. Maybe
they did have something in common after all.

In her embarrassment she'd temporarily forgotten about the
pain in her tummy, but the dragging feeling was back again
now so she took Georgette over to the sofa and sank down
gratefully. At the age of fourteen she'd fallen spectacularly
in love with Vidal, and known with fervent adolescent certainty that she would never find a man who could match him
in real life.

Her mouth twisted into an ironic smile. At fourteen everything seemed so black and white. At twenty-five, it was
all infinitely more complicated. Her teenage self had never
considered the possibility that she might meet her Vidal, only
for him to dismiss her as...

Her thoughts stalled as a piece of paper slid out of the book onto her knee.

Unfolding it, she saw straight away that it was a letter and felt a frisson of excitement. The date at the top was thirty years ago, the writing untidy, masculine and difficult to read, but she had no trouble making out the first line.

My Darling—

Technically Sophie was well aware that it was wrong to read other people's letters, but surely there was some kind of time limit on that rule? And anyway, any letter that began so romantically and was found in a Georgette Heyer novel was begging to be read. With a sense of delicious guilt she tucked her knees up tighter and scanned the lines.

It's late and the heat is just about bearable now the sun has gone down. I'm sitting on the roof terrace with the remains of the bottle of gin I brought back from England—I'd rather like to finish it all right now, but I couldn't bear the thought of Marie throwing the bottle away in the morning. It was the one we bought in London, that you held underneath your coat when we ran back to the hotel in the rain. How can I throw anything away that's been so close to your body?

Oh, how gorgeous! Sophie thought delightedly, trying to imagine Ralph writing something so intimate. Or doing anything as romantic as dashing through the rain to ravish the woman he loved in a hotel room.

Thank you, my love, for sending the photograph of K in your last letter. He's growing up so quickly—what happened to the plump baby I held in my arms on my last visit to Alnburgh? He is a boy now—a person in his own right, with a real character emerging—such fearless determination! Saying goodbye to him was so much harder this time. I never thought that anything would come close to the pain of leaving you, but at least your letters keep me going, and the memories of our time together. Leaving my son felt like cutting out a piece of myself.

Sophie's heart lurched and the written lines jumped before her eyes. Was K referring to Kit? Thirty years ago he must have been a small boy of three or four. Breathlessly she read on.

I suppose I've learned to accept sharing you with Ralph because I know you don't belong to him in any real sense, but the fact that K will grow up thinking of R as his father makes me rage against the injustice of everything.
Why couldn't I have found you first?

Her mouth had fallen open. Incredulously she read the lines again. After thirty years the sense of despair in them was still raw enough to make her throat close, but her brain couldn't quite accept the enormity of what she was reading.

Ralph Fitzroy wasn't Kit's father?

The sound of the door opening behind her made her jump about a mile in the air. Hastily, with trembling, nerveless fingers, she slid the letter back between the pages of Georgette Heyer and opened it randomly, pretending to read.

'Th-that was quick,' she stammered, turning round to see Kit come into the room carrying a bulging carrier bag. He was wearing the dark blue reefer jacket she remembered from the train and above the upturned collar his olive tan glowed with the cold. As he moved around the sofa he brought with him a sharp breath of outside—of frost and pine and ozone.

'I sensed that there was a certain amount of urgency involved.'

He put the bag down on the other end of the sofa and pulled out a huge box of tampons, which he tossed gently to her. Catching it, she couldn't meet his eye. The embarrassment of having him buy her sanitary products had paled into near-insignificance by the enormity of the discovery she'd just made.

'Thanks,' she muttered, looking round for her purse.

Taking off his jacket, he looked at her, slightly guarded. 'You're welcome. It's the least I could do for being so—' a frown appeared between his dark brows '—controlling. I'm sorry.'

'Oh, please—don't be,' Sophie said quickly. She meant it. The last thing she needed now was him standing here looking like the beautiful hero from an art-house film and being *nice*, wrenching open the huge crack that had appeared in her Kit-Fitzroy-proof armour after reading the letter.

He glanced at her in obvious surprise. 'I anticipated you'd be harder to make up to,' he said, delving back into the bag, pulling out the most enormous bar of chocolate. 'I thought this might be needed, at least. And possibly even this.' He held up a bottle.

'Gin?' Sophie laughed, though her heart gave another flip as she thought of the letter, and Kit's mother and her unknown lover drinking gin in bed while it poured down outside.

Oh, dear. Best not to think of bed.

Kit took the bottle over to a curved-fronted cupboard in the corner of the room behind the desk. 'Mrs Watts in the village shop, who under different circumstances would have had a brilliant career in the CID, looked at the other things I was buying and suggested that gin was very good for period pains.'

'Oh, God—I'm so sorry—how embarrassing for you.'

'Not at all, though I can't comment on the reliability of Mrs Watts's information.'

'Well, gin is a new one on me, but to be honest if someone suggested drinking bat's blood or performing naked yoga on the fourth plinth, I'd try it.'

'Is it that bad?' he said tonelessly, opening the cupboard and taking down a can of tonic water. Sophie watched the movements of his long fingers as he pulled the ring and unscrewed the gin bottle.

'N-not too bad this time. But sometimes it's horrendous. I mean, not compared to lots of things,' she added hastily, suddenly remembering that he was used to working in war zones, dealing with the aftermath of bombings. 'On a bad month it just makes it, you know...difficult.'

'There's some ibuprofen in the bag.' He sloshed gin into a glass. 'What does the doctor say?'

'I haven't seen one.' She wasn't even registered with one. She'd never really been in the same place for long enough, and Rainbow had always been a firm believer in remedies involving nettles and class B drugs. 'I looked it up on the Internet and I think it might be something called endometriosis. Either that, or one of twenty-five different kinds of terminal cancer—unlikely since I've had it for the last twelve years—appendicitis—ditto—or arsenic poisoning. I decided to stop looking after that.'

Kit came towards her, holding out a large glass, frosted with cold and clinking with ice cubes. 'You should see a doctor. But in the meantime try a bit of self-medicating.'

There was something about the sternness of his voice when combined with the faintest of smiles that made her feel as if she'd had a couple of strong gins already. Reaching up to take it from him, she felt herself blushing all over again.

'I don't have many unbreakable rules, but drinking hard spirits, on my own, in the middle of the morning is actually one I try to stick to. Aren't you having one too?' she said, then, realising that now he'd fulfilled his obligation he might be wanting to escape, added quickly, 'Unless you have something else you need to do, of course.'

'Not really. Nothing that won't keep anyway.' He turned away, picking up another log from the huge basket by the fireplace and dropping it into the glowing grate before going to pour another gin and tonic. 'I'm trying to go through some of the paperwork for the estate. It's in a hell of a mess. My father isn't exactly one for organisation. The whole place has been run on the ostrich principle for decades.'

'So Jasper gets his tendency to bury his head in the sand from Ralph?'

'I'm afraid so.' He sat down at the other end of the massive sofa, angling his body so he was facing her. 'And his tendency to drink too much and rely on charm to get him out of the more unpleasant aspects of life.' He broke off to take a large swig of his drink and shook his head. 'Sorry, I shouldn't be talking about him like that to you. To be fair, the womanising gene seems to have passed him by.'

'Yes.' Sophie's laugh went on a little too long. If only Kit knew the truth behind that statement. 'You're right, though. He and Ralph are astonishingly alike in lots of ways.'

She took a quick sip of her drink, aware that she was straying into dangerous territory. Part of her wanted desperately to ask him about the letter, or more specifically the shattering information it contained, but the rest of her knew she would never dare make such a personal assault on Kit Fitzroy's defences.

Silver eyes narrowed, he looked at her over the rim of his glass.

'Whereas I'm not like him at all.'

It was as if he had read her thoughts. For a moment she didn't know what to say, so she took another mouthful of gin and, nearly choking on it, managed to croak, 'Sorry. It's none of my business. I didn't—'

'It's fine.' Leaning back on the huge sofa, he tipped his head back wearily for a moment. 'It's no secret that my father and I don't get on. That's why I don't feel the need to spend every minute at his bedside.'

The room was very quiet. The only sounds were the hissing of the logs in the grate and the clink of ice in Sophie's glass as the hand that held it shook. Largely with the effort of stopping it reaching out and touching him

'Why?' she asked in a slightly strangled voice. 'Why don't you get on with him?'

He shrugged. 'It's always been like that. I don't remember having much to do with him before my mother left, and after she went you'd have thought we would have been closer.'

'Weren't you?'

'Exactly the opposite. Maybe he blamed me.' Kit held up his glass, looking through it dispassionately. The fire turned the gin the colour of brandy. 'Maybe he didn't, and just took it out on me, but what had previously been indifference became outright hostility. He sent me to boarding school at the soonest possible opportunity.'

'Oh, God, you poor thing.' Just thinking of her own brief boarding school experience made Sophie's scalp prickle with horror.

'God, no. I loved it. I was the only kid in the dorm who used to dread holidays.' He took a mouthful of gin, his face deadpan as he went on, 'He used to call me into the drawing room on my first evening home and go through my report, seizing on anything he could—a mark dropped here, a team captaincy missed there—and commenting on it in this strange, sarcastic way. Unsurprisingly it made me more determined to try harder and do better.' He smiled wryly. 'So then he'd mock me for being too clever and on too many teams.'

Sophie's heart turned over. She could feel it beating against her ribs with a rapid, jerky rhythm. The book, with its outrageous secret folded between the pages, stuck up slightly from the sofa cushions just inches from her right hip.

'Why would he do that?'

'I have no idea,' Kit drawled softly. 'It would be nice to think that he just wasn't someone who liked children, or could relate to them, but his unbridled joy when Jasper came along kind of disproves that. Anyway, it hasn't scarred me for life or anything, and I gave up trying to work it out a long time ago.'

'But you keep coming back here,' Sophie murmured. 'I'm not sure I would.' She looked down at the crescent of lemon stranded on the ice cubes in the bottom of her glass, letting her hair fall over her face in case it gave away how much of a howling understatement that was.

'I come back because of Alnburgh,' he said simply. 'It might sound mad but the place itself is part of my family as much as the people who live in it. And Ralph's approach to looking after the castle has been similar to the way he looked after his sons.'

She lifted her head. 'What do you mean?'

'All or nothing—five thousand pounds for new curtains in the drawing room, while the roof goes unmaintained.'

Their eyes met. He gave her that familiar brief, cool smile, but his eyes, she noticed, were bleak. Compassion beat through her, mixing uneasily with the longing churning in her tender stomach. *I know why it is*, she wanted to blurt out. *I know why he was always vile to you, and it isn't your fault.*

The moment stretched. Their gazes stayed locked together. Sophie felt helpless with yearning. The heat from the fire seemed to be concentrated in her cheeks, her lips...

She jumped out of her skin as the phone rang.

Kit moved quickly. He got to his feet to answer it so he didn't have to lean across her.

'Alnburgh.' His voice was like ground glass.

Sophie's hands flew to her face, pressing against her burning cheeks with fingers splayed. Her heart was galloping. From miles away, his voice reduced to a tinny echo, she could just make out that it was Jasper on the phone.

'That's good,' said Kit tonelessly. Then, after a pause, 'Ask her yourself.'

He held out the phone. Sophie couldn't look at him as she took it.

'Soph, it's good news.' Jasper's voice was jubilant. 'Dad's regained consciousness. He's groggy and a bit breathless but he's talking, and even managed a smile at the pretty blonde nurse.'

'Jasper, that's wonderful!' Sophie spoke with as much warmth as possible, given what she'd just found out about Ralph Fitzroy. 'Darling, I'm so pleased.'

'Yes. Look, the thing is, neither Ma nor I want to leave him while he's like this, so I was wondering if you'd mind very much if we didn't come back for dinner? Will you be OK on your own?'

'Of course.' Unconsciously she found her gaze moving back to Kit. He was standing in front of the fire, head bent, shoulders tensed. 'Don't worry. I'll be fine.'

'The other thing is,' Jasper said apologetically, 'Ma gave Mrs Daniels the day off...'

Sophie laughed. 'Believe it or not, some of us have evolved to the stage where we can survive without staff. Now, go and give Ralph...my regards.'

Her smile faded quickly as she put the phone down. The room was quiet again, as if it were waiting.

'They're not coming back,' she said, trying to sound casual. 'He just wanted to check we'd be OK, since it's Mrs Daniels' day off and I'm not known for my culinary skills.' She gave a nervous laugh. 'Where's the nearest Indian takeaway?'

'Hawksworth.' Kit turned round. His face was blank. 'But forget takeaway. I don't know about you but I need to get away from here. Let's go out.'

CHAPTER TEN

It's not a date, it's not a date, it's not a date.

Sophie looked at herself sternly in the mirror as she yanked a comb roughly through her wet hair. After a walk on the beach this afternoon it had needed washing anyway. She wasn't making any special effort because she was going out for dinner with Kit.

Her stomach dipped. *Period pain*, she told herself.

It would be rude not to make a little bit of effort, and, after being shut up at Alnburgh for days without seeing a soul apart from the odd dog walker on the beach, it was actually pretty good to have an excuse to liven up her corpselike pallor with blusher and put on something that wasn't chosen solely for its insulating properties.

But what?

She stopped combing, and stood still, her mind running over the possibilities. She was sick and tired of jeans, but discounting them only left the black shroud, the vampire corset thing or the Chinese silk dress Jasper had ruled out for Ralph's party on the grounds that it was too sexy. Tapping a finger against her lip, she considered.

It's not a date...

Absolutely not. But she wasn't wearing the shroud. And the corset would look as if a she were meeting a client and charging for it. The Chinese silk it would have to be.

A wave of undeniable nervousness rolled through her and she had to sit down on the edge of the bed. She was being ridiculous, getting dressed up and wound up about a dinner arrangement that was based purely on practical and logical reasons. Jasper wasn't coming back, Mrs Daniels was away, neither of them could cook and they were both going stir-crazy from being cooped up in the castle for too long. Unlike every other dinner invitation she'd ever had, this one very definitely wasn't the opening move in a game that would finish up in bed.

No matter how fantastic she sensed going to bed with Kit Fitzroy would be.

Stop it, she told herself crossly, getting up and slapping foundation onto her flushed cheeks. This was nothing to do with sex. That look that had passed between them in the library earlier had *not* been the precursor to a kiss...a kiss that would have led to who-knew-what if the phone hadn't rung. *No.* It was about finally, miraculously putting their differences behind them. Talking. About her being there at a rare moment when he had needed to offload.

She sighed. The trouble was, in a lot of ways that felt a whole lot more special and intimate than sex.

Her hands were shaking so much it took three goes to get her trademark eyeliner flick right. Then there was nothing else to do but put on the Chinese silk dress. She shivered as the thick crimson silk slid over her body, pulling tight as she did up the zip.

'*It's not a date*,' she muttered one more time, pulling a severe face at her reflection in the little mirror above the sink. But her eyes still glittered with excitement.

In the library Kit put down the folder of Inland Revenue correspondence he'd been going through and looked at his watch.

Seven o'clock—his lip curled slightly—about three minutes later than the last time he'd checked.

He got up, stretching his aching back and feeling fleetingly glad that he didn't have a desk job. He felt stiff and tired and restless; frustrated from being inside all day and surrounded by papers. That was all it was. Nothing to do with the persistent throb of desire that had made concentrating on tax impossible, or the fact that his mind kept going back to that moment on the sofa just before the phone rang.

The moment when he had been about to kiss her. Again. Only this time it wouldn't have been because he was trying to prove anything or score points or catch her out, but because he wanted to. *Needed* to.

Letting out a ragged sigh, he ran his hands through his hair and down over his face.

What the hell was he doing asking her out to dinner?

He was looking after her for Jasper, that was all. Trying to make up a little for the unrelenting misery of her visit, and for boring her with his life story earlier.

Especially for that.

It wasn't a *date* or anything.

Grimly he turned the lights out in the library and strode through into the hall, rubbing a hand across his chin and feeling the rasp of stubble. As he went into the portrait hall he heard footsteps echoing on the stone stairs and looked up.

His throat closed and his heart sank. He had to clench his teeth together to stop himself from swearing.

Because she was beautiful. Undeniably, obviously, hit-you-between-the-eyes beautiful, and it was going to be impossible to sit across a table from her all evening and not be aware of that for every minute. She was wearing a dress of Chinese silk that hugged her body like a second skin, but was high-necked and low-hemmed enough to look oddly demure.

Her footsteps slowed. She was looking at him, her expression uncertain, and it struck him that she was waiting for his reaction.

Swiftly he cleared his throat, rubbing his jaw again to un-clench it. 'You look...great,' he said gruffly. He'd been about to say beautiful, but stopped himself at the last minute. It seemed too intimate.

'I'm way overdressed.' She'd come to a standstill halfway down the stairs and turned around, preparing to bolt back up again. 'I didn't really have anything else, but I can put on jeans—'

'No.'

The word came out more forcefully than he'd meant and echoed off the stone walls. Her eyes widened with shock, but she didn't move.

'You're fine as you are, and I'm starving. Let's just go, shall we?'

He took her to a restaurant in Hawksworth. Tucked away in a small courtyard off the market square, it had a low-beamed ceiling, a stone-flagged floor and fires burning in each of its two rooms. Candles stuck into old wine bottles flickered on every table, throwing uneven shadows on the rough stone walls. Thanks to these it was mercifully dark and Sophie felt able to relax a little bit in her too-smart dress.

'You were right,' she said brightly, studying the menu without taking in a single thing on it. 'It is good to be away from the castle. And it's good to be warm, too.'

The maître d', recognising Kit, had shown them to the best table in a quiet corner of the far room, next to the fire. Its warmth stole into Sophie's body, but somehow she couldn't stop herself from shivering.

'Alnburgh hasn't quite lived up to your expectations, then?' Kit asked dryly as he studied the wine list, and Sophie remembered that journey from the station in the back of the Bentley when she'd seen the castle for the first time.

'Let's just say I'm a big fan of central heating. When I was little I used to think that I wouldn't mind where I lived as long as it was warm.'

Oh, dear, that was a stupid thing to say. She looked down, picking bits of fossilised wax off the wine bottle candle-holder with a fingernail and hoping he wouldn't pick up the subject of when she was little. The last thing she wanted to talk about was her childhood.

Actually, come to think of it, there were quite a lot of things she didn't want to talk about. Or couldn't. She'd better not drink too much or she'd be letting skeletons, and Jasper, out of the closet by dessert time.

'So where *do* you live?' he asked, putting the menu down and looking at her directly.

'Crouch End.' Beneath his gaze she felt ridiculously shy. 'I share a flat with a girl called Jess. Or I did, but then I went to Paris for two months for the Resistance film and when I got back her boyfriend had moved in. I guess it might be time to look for somewhere else.'

'Would you move in with Jasper?'

She shook her head, suppressing a rueful smile as she imagined Sergio's reaction if she did. 'I love Jasper, but it's not—'

She stopped as the waitress appeared; a slim, dark-skinned girl who slid a pencil out of her casually piled up hair to take their order. Sophie, who couldn't remember a single thing from the menu, spotted linguine on the specials board behind Kit and ordered that, cursing herself almost instantly for choosing something so inelegant to eat.

No sooner had the waitress sauntered off with catwalk grace than the maître d' brought a dish of olives and the wine, pouring it into glasses the size of goldfish bowls with a great deal of theatre. Sophie's pulse went into overdrive as the incident in the wine cellar came rushing back to her. Looking away, she felt her cheeks flame and wondered if Kit was remembering the same thing.

When they were alone again he raised his glass and said, 'Go on.'

She made a dismissive gesture, deliberately choosing to misremember where she'd got up to. Jasper was probably one of the subjects best placed on the 'Avoid' list.

'So anyway, I'll probably be flat-hunting when I get back to London, unless I stick it out at Love Central until I find out if I've got the vampire film role, because that'll involve about four weeks' filming in Romania...' She picked up her glass and took a huge mouthful, just to shut herself up. The glass was even bigger than she thought and some of the wine dripped down her chin, reminding her even more painfully of the port.

'Is it a big part?'

Kit's voice was low. In contrast to her he was utterly relaxed, his face impassive in the firelight. But why wouldn't he be relaxed? she thought despairingly. He didn't have a thumping great crush to hide, as well as most of the truth about himself.

'No. Lots of scenes but not many lines, which is perfect—' She looked up at him from under her lashes with a grimace of embarrassment. 'The only downside is the costume. My agent is always sending me scripts for bigger parts, but I don't want to go down that route. I'm quite neurotic enough as it is.'

Aware that she was babbling again, she picked up an olive, putting it in her mouth and sucking the salty oil off her fingers while she steadied herself to continue. 'I love what I do now,' she said more slowly. 'It's fun and there's no pressure. I'm not trained or anything and I just fell into it by chance, but it means I get to travel and do interesting things, and pick up the odd useful skill too.'

The waitress arrived and set plates down between them before sauntering off again.

'Such as?'

Kit's eyes were heavy-lidded, dark-lashed, gleaming.

Sophie looked down, knowing for certain there was no way she was going to be able to eat linguine when her stomach was already in knots. She picked up her fork anyway.

'Let me see… Archery. You never know when you might have to face an invading army with only a bow and arrow—especially at Alnburgh. Milking a cow. Pole dancing. Artificial respiration.'

Kit looked up at her in surprise. 'You learned that through acting?'

'I did a season in a TV hospital drama series.' She wound ribbons of pasta around her fork, assuming a lofty tone. 'I'm surprised you don't remember it actually—it was the highlight of my career, until the scriptwriters decided to kill me off in a clifftop rescue scene in the Christmas episode instead of letting me go on to marry the consultant and do another series.'

His smile was sudden and devastating. The firelight had softened his face, smoothing away the lines of tension and disapproval, making him look less intimidating and simply very, very sexy.

'Were you disappointed?'

She shook her head. 'Not really. It was good money but too much like commitment.'

'What, marrying the consultant or doing another series?'

The low, husky pitch of his voice seemed to resonate somewhere inside her, down in the region of her pelvis.

'Both.'

* * *

The place had emptied and the waitress was looking bored and sulky by the time Kit eventually stood up, stooping slightly to avoid the low beams as he went to sort out the bill.

Sophie watched him, her mouth dry, her trembling hands tucked beneath her thighs on the wooden bench. The gaps in the conversation had got longer and more loaded, the undercurrents of meaning stronger. Or so it had felt to her. Maybe he had just run out of things to say to her?

They drove back in silence. The sky was moonless, and veils of mist swathed the castle like chiffon scarves, making it look oddly romantic. Sophie's hands were folded in her lap and she held herself very stiffly, as if she were physically braced against the waves of longing that were battering at her. In the light of the dashboard Kit's face was tense and unsmiling. She gave an inward moan of despair as she wondered if he'd been totally bored by the whole evening.

He pulled into the courtyard and got out of the car immediately, as if he was at pains to avoid drawing the evening out a moment longer than he had to. Sophie followed, misery and disappointment hitting her more forcefully than the cold. For all her self-lecturing earlier, she had secretly longed to break through the barriers of Kit's reserve and rekindle the spark of intimacy that had glowed so briefly between them.

She caught up with him at the top of the steps as he keyed in the number.

'Thank you for a lovely evening,' she said in an oddly subdued voice. 'It seems awful to have had such a good time when Jasper and Tatiana are at the hospital. I hope Ralph is OK.'

'Given the mess Alnburgh's finances are going to be in if he dies, I do too,' Kit said sardonically as he opened the door. Standing back to let her through, he rubbed a hand across his forehead. 'Sorry. I didn't mean it to sound like that.'

'I know.'

She stopped in front of him, instinctively reaching up to touch the side of his face.

He stiffened, and for a moment she felt a jolt of horror at the thought that she'd got it badly wrong *again*. But then he dropped his hand and looked at her, and in the split second before their mouths met she saw desire and despair there that matched her own. She let out a moan of relief as his lips touched hers, angling her head back and parting her lips as he took her face between his hands and kissed her.

It was as though he was doing something that hurt him. The kiss was hard but gentle at the same time, and the expression on his face as he pulled away was resigned—almost defeated. Arrows of anguish pierced Sophie's heart and she slid her hand round his neck, tangling her fingers in his hair as she pulled his head down again.

The door swung shut behind them, giving a bang that echoed through the empty halls. They fell back against it, Sophie pressing her shoulders against the ancient wood as her hips rose up to meet his. Her hands slid over the sinews of his back, feeling them move as their bodies pressed together and their mouths devoured each other in short, staccato bursts of longing.

'Soph? Soph, darling, is that you?'

'Jasper,' she whimpered.

Kit pulled away, jerking his head back as if he'd been struck. They could hear footsteps approaching across the stone flags of the hall. Beneath the light of the vast lantern high above, Kit's face looked as if it had been carved from ice.

Helplessly Sophie watched him turn away, then, smoothing her skirt down, she went forwards, willing her voice not to give her away.

'Yes, it's me. We didn't expect you back so…'

Her words trailed off as Jasper appeared in the doorway.

His face was swollen and blotched from crying, and tears still slid from his reddened eyes.

'Oh, my darling—' she gasped.

Jasper raised his hands in a gesture of hopelessness. 'He died.'

And in an instant Sophie was beside him, taking him into her arms, stroking his hair as he laid his head on her shoulder and sobbed, murmuring to him in a voice that ached with love.

Over his shoulder she watched Kit walk away. She willed him to turn round, to look back and catch her eye and understand.

He didn't.

CHAPTER ELEVEN

AND SO, not quite a week after Ralph's lavish birthday party, preparations were made at Alnburgh for his funeral.

Kit returned to London the morning following Ralph's death. Sophie didn't see him before he left and though Thomas murmured something about appointments with the bank, Sophie, rigid with misery she couldn't express, wondered if he'd gone deliberately early to avoid her.

She was on edge the whole time. It felt as if her heart had been replaced with an alarm clock, like the crocodile in *Peter Pan*, making her painfully aware of every passing second. The smallest thing seemed to set her alarm bells jangling.

The bitter weather continued. The snow kept falling; brief, frequent flurries of tiny flakes that were almost invisible against the dead sky. Pipes in an unused bathroom burst, making water cascade through the ceiling in a corner of the armoury hall and giving the pewter breastplates their first clean in half a century. Thomas, who since Ralph's death seemed to have aged ten years, shuffled around helplessly, replacing buckets.

After that time in the hall Sophie didn't see Jasper cry again, but his grief seemed to turn in on itself and, without the daily focus of sitting at Ralph's bedside and the hope of his recovery to cling to, he quietly went to pieces. He was haunted by regret that he hadn't had the courage to come out about his sexuality to his father, driven to despair by the knowledge that now it was too late.

Sophie's nerves were not improved by a lonely, insecure Sergio ringing the castle at odd hours of the day and night and demanding to speak to Jasper. She fielded as many of the calls as possible. Now was not the time for the truth, but the charade had come to seem pointless and the main difficulty in Jasper and Sergio's relationship was not that it was homosexual but that Sergio was such an almighty, selfish prima donna.

On the occasions when Jasper did speak to Sergio he came off the phone with hollow eyes and a clenched jaw, and proceeded to get drunk. That was something else Sophie was worried about. It was becoming harder to ignore the fact that as the days wore on he was waking up later and making his first visit to the drinks tray in the library earlier.

But there was no one she could talk to about it. Tatiana barely emerged from her room, and Sophie sensed that speaking to Mrs Daniels or Thomas, as staff, would break some important social taboo. Of course, it was Kit that she really longed to talk to, but even if he had been there what could she say? Unless she was prepared to break Jasper's confidence, any concerns she expressed about his welfare would only serve to make Kit think more badly of her. Who could blame Jasper for drinking too much when his girlfriend had been about to leap into bed with his brother, while he was with his dying father?

As the week dragged on she missed him more and more. She even found herself counting the days to the funeral, where she knew she would see him again.

Looking forwards to a funeral, she told herself bleakly, was a mark of a truly bad person.

The day before the funeral Sophie was perched on top of a stepladder in the armoury hall. Taking down the antique pistols that had got soaked in the burst-pipe deluge, she dried them, one by one, as Thomas was anxious that, left alone, the mechanisms would rust. Sophie was very glad to have something to occupy her while Jasper huddled on the drawing room sofa, mindlessly watching horseracing.

Her roots were beginning to come through, and what she would really have liked to do was disappear into the bathroom with a packet of hair dye, but there was a line of shallowness that even she couldn't bring herself to cross. Anyway, the pistol-cleaning was curiously therapeutic. Close up, many of them were very beautiful, with delicate filigree patterns engraved into their silver barrels. She held one up to the light of the wrought-iron lantern, feeling the weight of it in her hand and wondering under what circumstances it had last been fired. A duel, perhaps, between two Fitzroy brothers, fighting over some ravishing aristocratic virgin.

The despair that was never far away descended on her again, faster than the winter twilight. If she was ravishing, or aristocratic—or a virgin for that matter—would Kit feel enough for her to want to fight for her?

Theatrically she pressed the barrel of the gun to her ribs, just below her breasts. Closing her eyes, she imagined him standing in front of her, in tight breeches and a ruffled white muslin shirt, his face tormented with silent anguish as he begged...

'Don't do it.'

Her eyes flew open. Kit was standing in the doorway, his face not tormented so much as exhausted. Longing hit her first—the forked lightning before the rumble of scarlet embarrassment that followed.

'Tell me,' he drawled coolly, picking up the stack of letters that had come in the last few days, 'had you considered suicide before, or is it being here that's driven you to make two attempts in the last week?'

Sophie made an attempt at a laugh, but it dried up in her throat and came out as a sort of bitter rasp. 'It must be. I was perfectly well adjusted before. How was your trip?'

'Frustrating.'

He didn't look up from the envelopes he was sifting through. Sophie averted her eyes in an attempt not to notice how sexy he looked, especially from her vantage point where she could see the breadth of his shoulders and the way his hair curled into the back of his neck, however, her nipples tingled in treacherous recognition. She stared at the pistol in her hand, polishing the barrel with brisk strokes of the cloth.

'I expect you'll be going back to London yourself when the funeral's over,' he said absently, as if it were of no consequence to him.

'Oh.' The idea had come out of the blue and she felt suddenly disorientated, and a little dizzy up there on the ladder. She took a quick breath, polishing harder. 'Yes. I expect so. I hadn't really thought. Are you going to be staying here for a while?'

He took one letter from the pile and threw the rest down again. 'No. I'm going back.'

'To London?'

To give her an excuse not to look at him she put the gun back on its hooks on the wall, but her hands were shaking and it slipped from her fingers. She gave a cry of horror, but with lightning reactions Kit had stepped forwards and caught it.

'Careful. There's a possibility that some of these guns might still be loaded,' he said blandly, handing it back to her. 'No. Not London. Back to my unit.'

For a moment the pain in Sophie's chest felt as if the gun *had* gone off.

'Oh. So soon?'

'There's not much I can do here.' For the first time their

eyes met and he gave a brief, bitter smile. 'And at least it's a hell of a lot warmer out there.'

Sophie's heart was thumping hard enough to shake the stepladder. She could tell from his offhand tone and his abstracted expression that he was about to walk away, and she didn't know when she would see him alone again, or get the chance to say any of the millions of things that flooded her restless head at night when sleep wouldn't come and she lay awake burning for him.

'I only came back to pick this up.' He held up the letter. 'I have an appointment with Ralph's solicitor in Hawksworth, so—'

'Kit—wait.' She jumped down from the stepladder, which was a bit higher than she thought, and landed unsteadily in front of him so he had to reach out a hand to grab her arm. He withdrew it again immediately.

Sophie's cheeks flamed. 'The other night—' she began miserably, unable to raise her head. 'I just wanted you to know that it wasn't a mistake. I knew what I was doing, and I—'

His eyes held a sinister glitter, like the frost outside. Beautiful but treacherous. 'Is that supposed to make it better?'

She shook her head, aware that it was coming out wrong. 'I'm trying to explain,' she said desperately. 'I don't want you to think that Jasper and I— It's not—we're not—'

Kit's mouth twisted into a smile of weary contempt. 'I'm not blaming *you* for what happened—it was just as much my fault. But I don't think either of us can really pretend it wasn't wrong.' Moving past her, he went to the huge arched door and put his hand on the iron latch. 'Like you, I don't have that many unbreakable rules but I wasn't aware until recently that one of them is that you don't touch your brother's woman. Under any circumstances.'

'But—'

'Particularly not just because you're both bored and available.'

The cruelty of his words made her incapable of reply. The door gave its graveyard creak as he opened it and went out, leaving nothing but an icy blast of winter in his wake.

The windscreen wipers beat in time to the throbbing in Kit's head, swiping the snow from in front of his eyes. But only for a minute. No sooner was the glass clear than more snow fell, obscuring everything again.

It seemed hideously symbolic of everything else in his life right now.

In London, trying to make some sense of Alnburgh's nightmarishly complicated legal and financial position, he had come up against nothing but locked doors and dead ends. But at least there he had had some perspective on the situation with Sophie.

Being back within touching distance of her had blown it all out of the water again.

Was it her acting ability or the way she looked up at him from under her eyelashes, or the fact that watching her rub the barrel of that gun had almost made him pull her down off the ladder and take her right there, against the door, that made him want to believe her? Wanted to make him accept it without question when she said that a little thing *like being Jasper's girlfriend* was no obstacle to them sleeping together?

He pulled up in the market square and switched the car engine off. For a moment he just sat there, staring straight ahead without seeing the lit-up shops, the few pedestrians, bundled up against the weather as they picked their way carefully over the snowy pavements.

Since his mother had left when he was six years old, Kit had lived without love. He didn't trust it. He had come to realise that he certainly didn't need it. Instead he had built his life on principles. Values. Moral codes. They were what informed his choices, not *feelings*.

And they were what he had to hold on to.

He got out of the car and slammed the door with unnecessary force and headed for the offices of Baines and Stanton.

The Bull was beginning to fill up with after-work drinkers when Kit came out of his meeting with the solicitor. He knocked back his first whisky in a single mouthful standing at the bar, and ordered another, which he took to a table in the corner.

He intended to be there for a while; he might as well make himself comfortable. And inconspicuous. On the wall opposite he noticed the Victorian etching of Alnburgh Castle. It looked exactly the same now as it had done a hundred years ago, he thought dully. Nothing had changed at all.

Apart from the fact it was no longer anything to do with him because *Ralph Fitzroy wasn't his father.*

It was funny, he thought, frowning down into the amber depths of his glass, several whiskies later. He was a bomb-disposal expert, for God's sake. He was trained to locate explosives and disarm them before they did any damage, and all the time he'd been completely oblivious to the great big unexploded bombshell in the centre of his own life.

It explained everything, he mused as the whisky gave a sort of warm clarity to his thoughts. It explained why Ralph had been such a spiteful *bastard* when he was growing up. And why he had always refused to discuss the future of the estate. It explained…

He scowled, struggling to fit in the fact that his mother had left him with a man who wasn't his father, and failing.

Oh, well, it explained some things. But it changed everything.

Everything.

He stood up, his chest suddenly tight, his breath clogging in his throat. Then, draining his whisky in one mouthful, left the bar.

Wrapped in a towel, still damp from the bath, Sophie put her bag on the bed and surveyed the contents in growing dismay.

Out of long habit she hadn't ever bothered to unpack, so she couldn't, even for a moment, enjoy a glimmer of hope that there might be something she'd temporarily forgotten about hanging in the wardrobe. Something smart. And black. And suitable for a funeral.

Black she could do, she thought, rifling through the contents of her case, which was like a Goth's dressing up box. It was smart and suitable where she fell down.

Knickers.

How could she have been so stupid as to spend most of the day looking for displacement activities and polishing pistols when she could have nipped out to The Fashion Capital of the North, which must surely do an extensive range of funeral attire? But it was way too late now. And she was pretty much left with one option.

She'd balled her last unlucky purchase from Braithwaite's in the bottom of the bag, from whence she'd planned to take it straight to the nearest charity shop when she got back to London, but she pulled it out again now and regarded it balefully. It was too long obviously, but if she cut it off at the knee and wore it with her black blazer, it might just do…

Rubbing herself dry, she hastily slipped on an oversized grey jumper of Jasper's and some thick hiking socks and set off downstairs. It was late. Tatiana had retired to her room ages ago and had supper on a tray, Thomas had long since gone back to his flat in the gatehouse and Sophie had helped a staggering, slightly incoherent Jasper to bed a good hour ago, after he had fallen asleep on the sofa watching *The Wizard of*

Oz. However, the fact that all the lights were still on down-stairs suggested Kit hadn't come back yet.

Her heart gave an uneven thud of alarm. Passing through the portrait hall, she looked at the grandfather clock. It was almost midnight. Kit had said something about him going to see the solicitor—surely he should have been back hours ago?

Visions of icy roads, twisted metal, blue lights zigzagged through her head, filling her with anguish. How ridiculous, she told herself grimly, switching the light on to go down the kitchen steps. It was far more likely that he'd met some old flame and had gone back to her place.

The anguish of that more realistic possibility was almost worse.

She switched the kitchen light on. On the long table in the centre of the room a roast ham and roast joint of beef stood under net domes, waiting to be sliced up for the buffet at the funeral tomorrow. After that she'd be going back to London, and Kit would be leaving for some dusty camp somewhere in the Middle East.

Sophie felt her throat constrict painfully.

She'd probably never see him again. After all, she'd been friends with Jasper all these years without meeting him. She remembered the photo in the paper and wondered if she'd catch glimpses of him on the news from time to time. A horrible thought struck her: please, God, not in one of those reports about casualties—

She jumped as she heard a noise from the corridor be-hind her. It was a sort of rusty grating; metal against metal: the noise made by an old-fashioned key being turned in a lock—yet another piece from Alnburgh's archive of horror-film sound effects. Sophie turned around, pressing herself back against the worktop, the scissors held aloft in her hand—as if that would help.

In the dark corridor the basement door burst open.

Kit stood there, silhouetted against the blue ice-light outside. He was swaying slightly.

'Kit.' Dropping the scissors, Sophie went towards him, concern quickening inside her. 'Kit, what happened? Are you OK?'

'I'm fine.'

His voice was harsh; as bleak and cold and empty as the frozen sky behind him.

'Where's the car?' Her heart was pumping adrenaline through her, making her movements abrupt and shaky as she stepped past him and slammed the door. In the light from the kitchen his face was ashen, his lips white, but his eyes were glittering pools of darkness.

'In town. Parked in the square outside the solicitor's office. I walked back.'

'Why?'

'Because I was well over the limit to drive.'

He didn't feel it. No gentle, welcome oblivion for him. The six-mile walk home had just served to sharpen his senses and give a steel-edged sharpness to every thought in his head.

And every step of the way he'd been aware of the castle, black and hulking against the skyline, and he'd known how every potential intruder, every would-be enemy invader, every outsider, for God's sake, for the last thousand years had felt when confronted with that fortified mass of rock.

One thought had kept him going forwards. The knowledge that the six-foot-thick walls and turrets and battlements contained Sophie. Her bright hair. Her quick smile. Her irreverence and her humour. Her sweet, willing body...

'What happened?'

She was standing in front of him now, trembling slightly. Or maybe shivering with the cold. She was always cold. He frowned down at her. She appeared to be wearing a large sweater and nothing else. Except thick woollen socks, which only seemed to make her long, slender legs look even more delicious. They were bare from mid-thigh downwards, which made it hard to think clearly about the question she'd just asked, or want to take the trouble to reply.

'Kit? Was it something the solicitor said?'

She touched his hand. Her skin was actually warm for once. He longed to feel it against his.

'Ralph wasn't my father.'

He heard his own voice say the words. It was hard and maybe, just maybe a tiny bit bitter. Damn. He didn't want to be bitter.

'Oh, Kit—'

'None of this is mine,' he said, more matter-of-factly now, walking away from her into the kitchen. He turned slowly, looking around him as if seeing it all for the first time.

'It all belongs to Jasper, I suppose. The castle, the estate, the title…'

She had come to stand in the doorway, her arms folded tightly across her chest. She was looking up at him, and her eyes were liquid with compassion and understanding and…

'I don't.'

Her voice low and breathless and vibrating with emotion as she came towards him. 'I want you to know that I don't belong to Jasper. I don't belong to *anyone*.'

'And I don't have a brother any more.'

For a moment they stared at each other wordlessly. And then he caught her warm hand in his and pulled her forwards, giving way to the onslaught of want that had battered at his defences since she'd sat down opposite him on the train.

Together they ran up the stairs, pausing halfway up at the turn of the staircase to find each other's mouths. Kit's face was frozen beneath Sophie's palms and she kissed him as if the heat of her longing could bring the warmth back into his body. His jaw was rough with stubble, his mouth tasted of whisky and as he slid his hands up beneath the sweater she gasped at the chill of his hands on her bare breasts while almost boiling over with need.

'God, Sophie...'

'Come on.'

Seizing his hand, she ran onwards, up the rest of the stairs. Desire made her disorientated, and at the top she turned right instead of left, just as she had that first night. Realising her mistake, she stopped, but before she could say anything he had taken her face in his hands and was pushing her up against the panelled wall, kissing her until she didn't care where they were, just so long as she could have him soon.

Her hips ground helplessly against him, so she could feel the hardness of his erection beneath his clothes.

'My room,' she moaned. 'It's the other way—'

'Plenty more.' He growled against her mouth and, without taking his lips from hers, felt along the panelling for the handle of the door a few feet away. As it opened he levered himself away from the wall and stooped to hoist her up against him. She wrapped her legs tightly around his waist as he carried her forwards.

Sophie wasn't sure if this was the same room she'd stumbled into on her first night, or another one where the air was damp and the furniture draped in dust sheets. The window was tall, arched, uncurtained, and the blue light coming through it gleamed dully on the carved oak posts of an enormous bed.

As he headed towards it her insides turned liquid with lust. The room was freezing, but his breath was warm against her breasts, making her nipples harden and fizz. He was still dressed, the wool of his jacket rough and damp against her thighs. As she slid out of his arms and onto the hard, high bed she pulled it off his shoulders.

She was on her knees on the slippery damask bedspread

and he stood in front of her. His face was bleached of colour, its hard contours thrown into sharp relief, his heavy-lidded eyes black and fathomless.

He was so beautiful.

Her breath caught. Her hands were shaking as she reached out to undo the buttons of his shirt. He closed his eyes, tipping his head back, and Sophie could see the muscles quilt in his jaw as he fought to keep control.

It was one battle he wasn't going to win.

Gently now, she slid her hands beneath his open shirt, feeling him flinch with his own raw need. His skin still felt chilled. Tenderness bloomed and ached inside her, giving her desire a poignancy that scared her. She felt as if she were dancing, barefoot, free, but right on the edge of a precipice.

His shirt fell away and quickly she peeled off her jumper. Slowly, tightly, she wrapped her arms around him, pressing her warm, naked body against his cold one, cradling his head, kissing his mouth, his cheekbones, his eyes, his jaw as he lowered her onto the bed.

His heartbeat was strong against her breasts. Their ribs ground together as he undid his jeans with one hand and kicked them off. Sophie reached up and yanked at the damask cover so she could pull it over them, to warm him again. She was distantly aware of its musty smell, but she couldn't have cared less because he was cupping her cheek, trailing the backs of his fingers with exquisite, maddening lightness over her breast until her nerves screamed with desperation.

Reality blurred into a dreamlike haze where she was aware of nothing but his skin against hers, his breath in her ear, his lips on her neck. She kept her eyes fixed on his, swimming in their gleaming depths as beneath the sheets his hands discovered her body.

And with each stroke of his palm, each well-placed brush of his fingers she was discovering herself. Sex was something she was relaxed about, comfortable with. She knew what she was doing, and she enjoyed it. It was *fun*.

And this was as far removed from anything she'd ever felt before as silk was from sackcloth. This wasn't fun, it was essential. As he entered her, gently, deeply, she wasn't sure if it was more like dying or being born again.

Her cry of need hung in the frigid air.

She had never known anything more perfect. For a moment they were both still, adjusting to the new bliss of being joined together, and, looking into his eyes, she wanted to make it last for ever.

But it was impossible. Her body was already crying out for more, her hips beginning to move of their own accord, picking up their rhythm from him. His thumb brushed over her lips, and she caught it between her teeth as with the other hand he found her clitoris, moving his fingertip over it with every slow, powerful thrust.

The thick, ages-old silence of the room pooled around them again. The massive bed was too strong to creak as their bodies moved. Sophie wanted to look at him for ever. She wanted to hold for a lifetime the image of his perfect face, close to hers, as she spiralled helplessly into the most profound chasm of sensation. Their legs were entwined, his muscles hard against hers, and she didn't know where he ended and she began.

She didn't know anything any more. As a second cry—her high, broken sob of release—shattered the stillness she could only feel that everything she'd ever thought she believed was ashes and dust.

Kit slept.

Whether it was the whisky or the six-mile walk or the shattering, deathlike orgasm he didn't know, but for the first time in years he slept like the angels.

He woke as the sun was coming up, streaking the sky with

rose-pink ribbons and filling the room with the melting light of dawn. In his arms Sophie slept on, her back pressed against his chest, her bottom warm and deliciously soft against his thighs.

Or, more specifically, against his erection.

Gritting his teeth, he willed it away as remorse began to ebb through him, dissolving the haze of repletion and leaving him staring reality in the face. He closed his eyes again, not wanting to look at reality, or at Sophie, whose vibrant beauty had an ethereal quality in the pink half-light. As a way of blotting out the anger and the hurt and the shock of his discovery, last night had been perfect—more than he could have hoped for, and certainly more than he deserved. But it was a one-off. It couldn't happen again.

Sophie stirred in his arms, moving her hips a fraction, pressing herself harder against the ache of his erection. He bit back a moan, dragging his mind back from the memories of her unbuttoning his shirt, wrapping her arms around him and holding him when he most needed to be held, folding herself around him as he entered her...

The whisky might have blunted the pain and temporarily short-circuited his sense of honour, but it hadn't dulled his memory. Every detail was there, stored and ready for instant replay in the back of his head. A fact that he suspected was going to prove extremely inconvenient in the nights ahead when he was alone in a narrow bunk, separated from the rest of his men by the thinnest of makeshift walls.

Rolling out of bed, he picked his jeans up from the floor and pulled them on. The pink light carried an illusion of warmth, but the room was like a fridge and he had to clench his teeth together to stop them chattering as he reached into the sleep-warm depths of the bed and slid his arms under her.

She sighed as he gathered her up as gently as possible, but she didn't wake. Kit found himself fighting the urge to smile as he recalled the swiftness with which she'd fallen asleep on the train the first time he'd seen her, and the way it had both intrigued and irritated him. But, looking down into her face as he carried her down the shadowy corridor to her own room, the smile faded again. She was like no woman he'd ever known before. She'd appeared from nowhere, defiant, elusive, contradictory, and somehow managed to slip beneath his defences when he'd wanted only to push her away.

How had she done that?

With one shoulder he nudged open the door to her room. The window faced north, so no dawn sunlight penetrated here, and it was even colder, if that were possible, than the room they'd just left. It was also incredibly neat, he noticed with a flash of surprise, as if she was ready to leave at any moment. Her hair was fragrant and silken against his bare chest as he laid her gently down on the bed, rolling her sideways a little so he could pull back the covers and ease them over her.

Her eyes half opened as he tucked her in and she gazed up at him for a moment, her lips curving into a sleepy smile as she reached out and stroked the back of her hand down his midriff.

'It's cold without you,' she murmured. 'Come back.'

'I can't.' His voice was like sandpaper and he grasped her hand before it went any lower, his fingers tightening around hers for a moment as he laid it back on the bed. 'It's morning.'

She rolled onto her back and gave a little sighing laugh. 'It's over, you mean.'

'It has to be.' He pushed the heels of his hands into his eyes, physically stopping himself from looking at her as he spoke so his resolve wouldn't weaken. 'We can't change what we did last night, but we can't repeat it either. We just need to get through today without giving Jasper any reason to suspect.'

Against the pillow her face was still and composed, her hair spilling around it and emphasising its pallor. She closed her eyes.

'OK.'

The small, resigned word wasn't what he had expected and it pushed knives of guilt into his gut. Why was she making him feel as if this were his fault? Last night they had both been reckless but the result was just the logical conclusion to everything that had happened between them since the moment they'd met. It had felt inevitable somehow, but nonetheless forbidden.

Kit turned away and walked to the door, bracing his arm against the frame before he opened it and saying with great weariness, 'Sophie, what did you expect?'

Her eyes opened slowly, and the smile she gave him was infinitely sad.

'Nothing,' she said softly. 'Nothing.'

After he'd gone Sophie rolled over and let the tears spill down her cheeks.

He had slept with her because he'd finally found a get-out clause in his moral rule book. He no longer had a duty to Jasper, and that made it OK for him. But what about her?

Last night she thought he understood, without making her spell it out, that she wasn't betraying Jasper by sleeping with him.

It seemed he didn't.

She hadn't expected for ever. She hadn't expected declarations of undying love. Only for him to trust her.

CHAPTER TWELVE

'THE cars are here, madam.'

Thomas appeared in the hallway, his face rigidly blank as he made his announcement. But Sophie heard the slight break in his voice and felt the lump of emotion in her throat swell a little.

She mustn't cry. Not when Tatiana was holding herself together with such dignity. Getting into the gleaming black Bentley, she was the picture of sober elegance in a narrow-fitting black skirt and jacket, her eyes hidden by a hat with a tiny black net veil. Jasper got in beside her. He was grey-faced, hollow-cheeked, a ghost of the languid, laughing boy she knew in London. She noticed his throat working as he glanced at the hearse in front, where Ralph's polished coffin lay decked in white flowers, and as he settled himself in the back of the car he had to twist his hands together to stop them shaking.

Poor Jasper. She had to stay strong for him. Today was going to be such an ordeal, and his grief was so much more profound than anything she'd ever experienced. She dug her nails into her palm. And anyway, what did she have to cry about? She'd hardly known Ralph. And it was stupid, *stupid* to be upset over a one-night stand with a man she wasn't going to see again after today.

'After you.'

She looked up and felt her knees buckle a little. Kit was standing behind her on the steps to the castle, his perfectly tailored black suit and tie cruelly highlighting his austere beauty. His face was completely expressionless, and his silver eyes barely flickered over her as he spoke.

His indifference was like knives in her flesh. It was as if last night had never happened.

'Oh. I'm not sure I should go in the official car,' she stammered, looking down at her shoes. 'I'm not family or anything.'

'That makes two of us,' he murmured acidly. 'You're Jasper's girlfriend, that's close enough. Just get in—unless you're planning to walk in those heels.'

She did as she was told, but without any of the grace with which Tatiana had performed the manoeuvre, and was aware that Kit would have got a very unflattering view of her bottom in the tight black dress. She wondered if he'd seen that the hem was stuck up with Sellotape where she'd hurriedly cut it off at the knee this morning and hadn't had time to sew it.

Further evidence of her lack of class. Another reason for him to put her in the category of 'Women to Sleep With' (subsection: Once) rather than 'Women to Date'.

He got in beside her and an undertaker with a permanent expression of compassionate respect shut the door. Sophie found herself huddling close to Jasper so she could leave an inch of cream leather seat between her leg and Kit's. As the car moved silently beneath the arched gateway she bit her lip and kept her head turned away from him, her gaze fixed out of the window. But she could still catch the faint dry, delicious scent of his skin and that was enough to make the memories of last night come flooding back. She wished she could switch them off, as Thomas had switched off the water supply when the pipe had burst. But even if she could, she thought sadly, her body would still remember and still throb with longing for him.

The rose-pink sunrise had delivered a beautiful winter's day for Ralph's send-off—crisp, cold and glittering, just like the day of his party. The leaden clouds of the last grim week had lifted to reveal a sky of clean, clear blue.

Outside the church of St John the Baptist people stood in groups, stamping their feet to keep warm as they talked. Some were smartly dressed in black, but most of them wore everyday outdoor gear, and Sophie realised they must be local people, drawn by the social spectacle rather than grief. They fell silent and turned sombre, curious faces towards them as the cars turned into the churchyard.

'I forgot to bring the monkey nuts,' muttered Jasper with uncharacteristic bitchiness.

'People are curious,' said Tatiana in a flat, cold voice. 'They want to see if we feel things differently from them. We don't, of course. The difference is we don't show our feelings.'

Sophie bit her lip. She was one of those people, with her cheap dress and her Sellotaped hem. She wasn't part of the 'we' that Tatiana talked about. She wasn't even Jasper's girlfriend, for pity's sake. As they got out of the car and Jasper took his mother's arm to escort her into the church, Sophie tried to slip to the back, looking for Thomas and Mrs Daniels to sit with. A firm hand gripped her arm.

'Oh, no, you don't,' said Kit grimly.

He kept hold of her arm as they progressed slowly down the aisle of the packed church, behind Tatiana and Jasper and the coffin. Torn between heaven and hell at his closeness, Sophie was aware of people's heads turning, curious eyes sweeping over her beneath the brims of countless black hats, no doubt wondering who she was and what right she had to be there. She felt a barb of anguish as she realised people must think she was with Kit.

If only.

'I am the resurrection and the life...'

Beside her Kit's hands were perfectly steady as he held his service sheet without looking at it. Sophie didn't allow herself to glance at him, but even so she knew that his gaze was fixed straight ahead and that his silver eyes would be hard and dry, because it was as if she had developed some supernatural power that made her absolutely instinctively aware of everything about him.

Was that what loving someone did to you?

She lifted her head and looked up at the stained-glass window above the altar. The winter sunlight was shining through it, illuminating the jewel-bright colours and making the saints' faces positively glow with righteousness. She smiled weakly to herself. It's divine retribution, isn't it? she thought. My punishment for playing fast and loose with the affections of Jean-Claude and countless others. For thinking I was above it all and being scornful about love...

There was a shuffling of feet as the organ started and the congregation stood up. Sophie hastily followed suit, turning over her service sheet and trying to work out where the words to the hymn were. She was aware of Kit, towering above her like some dark angel, as he handed her an open hymn book, tapping the right page with a finger.

'I vow to thee my country...'

It was a hymn about sacrifice. Numbly Kit registered the familiar lines about laying down your life for your nation and wondered what the hell Ralph knew about any of that. As far as Kit knew, Ralph had never put his own needs, his own desires anything but first. He had lived for pleasure. He had died, the centre of attention at his own lavish party, not alone and thousands of miles from home on some hot, dusty roadside.

He would never have sacrificed his happiness for the sake of his brother.

Was that yet another item on his list of character flaws, or evidence that he was a hell of a lot cleverer than Kit after all?

Kit let the hymn book in his hands drop and closed his eyes as the hymn reached its stirring climax. Everyone sat down again, and as Sophie moved beside him he caught a breath of her perfume and the warmth of her body on the arctic air.

Want whiplashed through him, so that he had to grip the back of the pew in front to steady himself. Kit had attended too many funerals, carried too many flag-draped coffins onto bleak airfields to be unaware that life was short. Rules and principles didn't help when you were dead.

Joy should be seized. Nights like the one he'd just spent with Sophie should be celebrated.

Shouldn't they?

In the elaborately carved pulpit supplied by another long-gone Fitzroy, the vicar cleared his throat and prepared to start his address. Kit forced himself to drag his attention away from Sophie's hands, resting in her lap. The skin was translucent pale against her black dress. They looked cold. He wanted to warm them, as she'd warmed him last night.

'We come together today to celebrate the life of Ralph Fitzroy, who to those gathered here was not just the Earl of Hawksworth, but a husband, father and friend.'

It was just sex. That was what she'd said on the phone the first time he'd seen her, wasn't it? Just sex. He had to forget it. Especially now, in the middle of a funeral...

'Let's just take a few moments of silent reflection,' the vicar encouraged, 'to enjoy some personal memories of Lord

Fitzroy, and reflect on the many ways in which he touched our lives...'

Ye Gods, thought Kit despairingly, rubbing at the tense muscles across his forehead. In his case, remembering the ways in which Ralph had touched his life really wasn't such a good idea. All around him he was aware of people reaching for tissues, sliding arms around each other in mutual support while he sat locked in the private dungeon of his own bitterness. Alone.

And then, very gently Sophie put her hand over his, lacing her cold fingers through his, caressing the back of his hand with her thumb with a touch that had nothing to do with sex, but was about comfort and understanding.

And he wasn't alone any more.

'Lovely service,' people murmured, dabbing their eyes as they filed out into the sharp sunlight to the strains of The Beatles singing 'In My Life'. That had been Jasper's idea.

'You OK?' Sophie asked him, slipping her arm through his as Tatiana was swept up in a subdued round of air-kissing and clashing hat brims.

'Bearing up.' He gave her a bleak smile. 'I need a drink.'

'What happens now?'

'We go back for the interment.' He shuddered. 'There's a Fitzroy family vault at Alnburgh, below the old chapel in the North Gate. It's tiny, and just like the location for a low-budget horror film, so I'll spare you that grisly little scene. Mum and I, and the vicar—and Kit too, I suppose—will do the honours, by which time everyone should have made their way back up to the castle for the drinks. Would you mind staying here and sort of shepherding them in the right direction?'

In spite of the sunshine the wind sweeping the exposed clifftop was like sharpened razor blades. Jasper was rigid with cold and spoke through clenched teeth to stop them chattering. Weight had dropped off him in the last week, Sophie noticed, but whether it was from pining for his father or for Sergio she wasn't sure. Reaching up, she pressed a kiss on his frozen cheek.

'Of course I will. Go and say your goodbyes.'

He got into the car beside Tatiana. 'Save a drink for me,' he said dismally. 'Don't let the hordes drink us dry.'

Sophie bent to look at him through the open door. 'Of course I will.'

She turned round. Kit was standing behind her, obviously waiting to get into the car, his eyes fixed on some point in the far distance rather than at her rear.

'Sorry.' Hastily Sophie stepped out of the way. 'Are you going to the interment too?' she added in a low voice.

A muscle twitched in his cheek. 'Yes. For appearance's sake. At some point Jasper and I need to have a proper talk, but today isn't the right time.' He looked at her, almost reluctantly, with eyes that were as bleak as the snow-covered Cheviots stretching away behind him. 'At some point you and I should probably talk too.'

An icy gust of wind whipped a strand of hair across Sophie's face. Moving her head to flick it out of the way again, a movement in the distance caught her eye. Someone was vaulting over the low wall that separated the graveyard from the road, loping towards them between the frosty headstones.

Oh, no... Oh, please, no... Not now...

Sophie felt the blood drain from her head. It was a familiar enough figure, although incongruous in this setting. A bottle of vodka swung from one hand.

'Today might not be the best time for that either,' she said, folding her arms across her chest to steady herself. 'You should go—I think they're waiting.'

It was an answer of sorts, Kit thought blackly as he lowered himself into the Bentley and slammed the door. Just not the one he'd hoped for.

As the car began to move slowly away in the wake of the hearse Kit watched her take a few steps backwards, and then turn and slip into the cluster of people left behind outside the church. He lost sight of her for a few seconds, but then caught a glimpse of her hair, fiery against the monochrome landscape. She was hurrying in the direction of someone walking through the churchyard.

'Such a lot of people,' said Tatiana vaguely, pulling her black gloves off. 'Your father had so many friends.'

Jasper put an arm around her. 'It was a great service. Even Dad, who hated church, would have enjoyed it.'

Kit turned his face to the window.

The man's clothes marked him out as being separate from the funeral-goers. He was dressed neither as a mourner nor in the waterproofs and walking boots of the locals, but in skintight jeans, some kind of on-trend, tailored jacket with his shirt tails hanging down beneath it. Urban clothes. There was a kind of defiant swagger to the man's posture and movements, as if he was doing something reckless but didn't care, and as the car waited to pull out onto the main road Kit watched in the wing mirror as Sophie approached him, shaking her head. It looked as if she was pleading with him.

The car moved again, and for a few seconds the view in the wing mirror was a blur of hedge and empty sky. Kit stared straight ahead. His hands were clenched into fists, his heart beating heavily in his chest.

He waited, counting the beats. And then, just before the bend in the road when the church would be out of sight, he turned and looked back in time to see her put her arms around him.

When she'd taken his hand in church like that, it had

changed something. Or maybe that was wrong—maybe it hadn't changed, so much as shown him what was there before that he hadn't wanted to admit.

That possibly what he wanted from her—with her—wasn't just sex. And the hope that, at some point, when she had settled things with Jasper, she might want that too.

It looked as if he'd been wrong.

'Please, Sergio. It won't be for long. A couple of hours—maybe three, just until the funeral is over.'

Sergio twitched impatiently out of her embrace. 'Three hours,' he sneered. 'You make it sound like nothing, but every hour is like a month. I've waited over a week already and I've just spent all day on a stupid train. I *need* him, Sophie. And he needs me.'

'I know, I know,' Sophie soothed, glancing back at the church with its dwindling crowd of mourners, and sending up a silent prayer for patience. Or, failing that, forgiveness for putting her hands round Sergio's elegant, self-absorbed neck and killing him.

What had Kit meant, they needed to talk? And why did bloody Sergio have to choose the very moment when she could have asked him to stage his ridiculous, melodramatic appearance?

'You don't,' Sergio moaned theatrically. 'Nobody knows.'

'I know that Jasper's in despair without you,' Sophie said with exaggerated patience. 'I know he misses you every second, but I also know that his mother needs him right now. And he needs to get closure on this before he can be with you properly.'

It was the right thing to say. 'Closure' was the kind of psychological pseudoscience that Sergio lapped up.

'Do you think so?'

'Uh-huh.' Sensing victory, Sophie took the bottle out of

his hand and began to lead him through the gravestones back in the direction from which he'd just come. 'And I also think that you're tired. You've had a horrible week and an exhausting journey. The pub in the village has rooms—why don't we see if they have anything available and I'll tell Jasper to join you there as soon as he can? It would be better than staying at the castle, just for now.'

Sergio cast a wistful glance up at Alnburgh Castle, its turrets and battlements gilded by the low winter sun. Sophie sensed rebellion brewing and increased her pace, which wasn't easy with her heels snagging into the frosty grass. 'Here—I'll come with you and make sure you're settled,' she said firmly. 'And then I'll go to Jasper and tell him where you are.'

Sergio took her arm and gave it a brief, hard squeeze, in the manner of a doomed character in a war film. His blue eyes were soulful. 'Thank you, Sophie, I do as you say. I *trust* you.'

The hallway was filled with the sound of voices and a throng of black-clad people, many of whom had been here only a week earlier for Ralph's party. After the surreal awfulness of the little scene in the Alnburgh vault Kit felt in desperate need of a stiff drink, but he couldn't go more than a couple of paces without someone else waylaying him to offer condolences, usually followed by congratulations on the medal.

His replies were bland and automatic, and all the time he was aware of his heart beating slightly too fast and his body vibrating with tension as he surreptitiously looked around for Sophie.

'Your father must have been immensely proud of you,' said an elderly cousin of Ralph's in an even more elderly fur coat. The statement was wrong in so many ways that for a moment Kit couldn't think what could have prompted her to make it. 'For the George Medal,' she prompted, taking a sip of sherry and looking at him expectantly.

It was far too much trouble to explain that such was his father's indifference that he hadn't told him. Oh, and that he wasn't actually his father either. Instead he gave a neutral smile and made a polite reply before excusing himself and moving away.

Conversation was impossible when there was so much that he couldn't say. To anyone except Sophie.

He had to find her.

'Kit.'

The voice was familiar, but unexpected. Feeling a hand on his arm, Kit looked around to see a large black hat and, beneath it, looking tanned, beautiful but distinctly uneasy, was Alexia.

'Darling, I'm so sorry,' she murmured, holding on to her hat with one hand as she reached to kiss each of his cheeks. 'Such a shock. You must all be devastated.'

'Something like that. I wasn't expecting to see you here.'

Kit knew that his voice suggested that the surprise wasn't entirely a pleasant one, and mentally berated himself. It wasn't Alexia's fault he'd seen Sophie falling into the arms of some tosser in a girl's jacket amongst the headstones, or that she'd subsequently disappeared.

'Olympia and I were in St Moritz last weekend, but when her mother told us what happened I just wanted to be here. For you, really. I know I wasn't lucky enough to know your father well, but...' Beneath her skiing tan her cheeks were pink. 'I wanted to make sure you're OK. I still care about you, you know...'

'Thanks.'

She bent her head slightly, so the brim of her hat hid her face, and said quietly, 'Kit—it must be a horrible time. Don't be alone.'

Kit felt a great wave of despair wash over him. What was this, International Irony Day? For just about the first time in his life he didn't *want* to be alone, but the only person he wanted to be with didn't seem to share the feeling.

'I'll bear that in mind,' he said wearily, preparing to make his escape. And no doubt he would, but not in the way she meant.

'Hello, Kit—so sorry about your father.'

If they were standing in the armoury hall, Kit reflected, at this point he would have had difficulty stopping himself grabbing one of the pistols so thoroughly polished by Sophie and putting it against his head. As it was he was left with no choice but to submit to Olympia Rothwell-Hyde's over-scented embrace and muster a death-row smile.

'Olympia.'

'Ma said you were an absolute *god* at the party, when it happened,' she said, blue eyes wide with what possibly passed for sincerity in the circles she moved in. 'Real heroic stuff.'

'Obviously not,' Kit said coolly, glancing round, 'since we find ourselves here…'

Olympia, obviously unaware that it was International Irony Day, wasn't thrown off her stride for a second. Leaning forwards, sheltering beneath the brim of Alexia's hat like a spy in an Inspector Clousseau film, she lowered her voice to an excited whisper.

'Darling, I have to ask… That redhead you sat next to in church. She looks terribly like a girl we used to know at school called Summer Greenham, but it *can't* be—'

Electricity snapped through him, jolting him out of his apathy.

'Sophie. She's called *Sophie* Greenham.'

'Then it *is* her!' Olympia's upper-crust voice held a mixture of incredulity and triumph as she looked at Alexia. 'Who can blame her for ditching that embarrassing drippy hippy name? She should have changed her surname too—apparently it came from the lesbian peace camp place. Anyway, darling, none of that explains what she's *doing* here. Does she work here, because if so I would *so* keep an eye on the family silver—'

'She's Jasper's girlfriend.' Maybe if he said it often enough he'd accept it.

'No way. No. *Way!* Seriously? Ohmigod!'

Kit stood completely still while this pantomime of disbelief was going on, but beneath his implacable exterior icy bursts of adrenaline were pumping through his veins.

'Meaning?'

Beside Olympia, Alexia shifted uneasily on her designer heels. Olympia ploughed on, too caught up in the thrill of gossip to notice the tension that suddenly seemed to crackle in the air.

'She came to our school from some filthy traveller camp— an aunt took pity on her and wanted to civilise her before it was too late, or something. Whatevs.' She waved a dismissive hand. 'Total waste of money as she was expelled in the end, for stealing.' She took a sip of champagne before continuing in her confident, bitchy drawl. 'It was just before the school prom and a friend of ours had been sent some money by her mother to buy a dress. Well, the cash disappeared from the dorm and suddenly—by astonishing coincidence—Miss Greenham-Extremely-Common, who had previously rocked the jumble-sale-reject look, appears with a *very* nice new dress.'

A pulse was throbbing in Kit's temple. 'And you put two and two together,' he said icily.

Olympia looked surprised and slightly indignant. 'And reached a very obvious four. Her aunt admitted she hadn't given her any money—I think the fees were quite enough of a stretch for her—and the only explanation Summer could give was that her mother had bought it for her. Her mother who lived on a *bus*, and hadn't been seen for, like, a *year* or something and so was conveniently unavailable for comment, having nothing as modern as a *telephone*…'

Looking down at the floor, Kit shook his head and gave a soft, humourless laugh. 'And therefore unavailable to back her up either.'

'Oh, come on, Kit,' said Olympia, in the kind of jolly, dismissive tone that suggested they were having a huge joke and he was spoiling it. 'Sometimes you don't need *evidence* because the truth is so obvious that everyone can see it. And anyway—' she gave him a sly smirk from beneath her blonde flicky fringe '—if she's Jasper's girlfriend, why would she have just been checking into a room in the pub in the village with some bloke? Alexia and I went for a quick drinkie to warm ourselves up after the service and saw her.' The smirk hardened into a look of grim triumph. 'Room three, if you don't believe me.'

If Sophie had known she was going to walk back from the village to the castle in the snow, she would have left the shag-me shoes at home and worn something more sensible.

It was just as well her toes were frozen, since she suspected they'd be even more painful if they weren't. Unfortunately even the cold couldn't anaesthetise the raw blisters on her heels and it was only the thought of finding Kit, hearing what it was he had to say that kept her going.

She also had to find Jasper and break the news to him that Sergio had turned up. Having ordered an enormous break-fast for him to mop up some of the vodka and waited to make sure he ate it, she had finally left him crashed out on the bed. He shouldn't be any trouble for the next hour or so, but now the formal part of the funeral was over she knew that Jasper wouldn't want to wait to go and see him. And also she was guiltily keen to pass over the responsibility for him to Jasper as soon as possible. Sitting and listening to him endlessly talking about his emotions, analysing every thought that had flickered across his butterfly brain in the last week had made her want to start on the vodka herself. She had found herself thinking wistfully of Kit's reserve. His understatement. His emotional integrity.

Gritting her teeth against the pain, she quickened her steps.

The drive up to the castle was choked with cars. People had obviously decided they were staying for a while, and parked in solid rows, making it impossible for anyone to leave. Weaving through them, Sophie could hear the sound of voices spilling out through the open door and carrying on the frosty air.

Her heart was beating rapidly as she went up the steps, and it was nothing to do with the brisk walk. She paused in the armoury hall, tugging down her jacket and smoothing her skirt with trembling hands, noticing abstractedly that the Sellotaped hem was coming down.

'Is everything all right, Miss Greenham?'

Thomas was standing in the archway, holding a tray of champagne, looking at her with some concern. Sophie realised what a sight she must look in her sawn-off dress with her face scarlet from cold and exertion, clashing madly with her hair.

'Oh, yes, thank you. I just walked up from the village, that's all. Do you know where Jasper is?'

'Master Jasper went up to his room when he got back from the interment,' said Thomas, lowering his voice respectfully. 'I don't think he's come down yet.'

'OK. Thanks. I'll go up and see if he's all right.' She hesitated, feeling a warm blush gather in her already fiery cheeks. 'Oh, and I don't suppose you know where I could find Kit, do you?'

'I believe he's here somewhere,' Thomas said, turning

round creakily, putting the champagne glasses in peril as he surveyed the packed room behind him. 'I saw him come in a little while ago. Ah, yes—there he is, talking to the young lady in the large hat.'

Of course, he was so much taller than everyone else so it wasn't too hard to spot him. He was standing with his back half to her, so she couldn't see his face properly, only the scimitar curve of one hard cheekbone. A cloud of butterflies rose in her stomach.

And then she saw who he was talking to. And they turned into a writhing mass of snakes.

CHAPTER THIRTEEN

A CHILDHOOD spent moving around, living in cramped spaces with barely any room for personal possessions, being ready to move on at a moment's notice, had left its mark on Sophie in many ways. One of them was that she travelled light and rarely unpacked.

Once she'd seen Jasper it didn't take her long to get her few things together. It took a little longer to get herself together, but after a while she felt strong enough to say goodbye to her little room and slip along the corridor to the back staircase.

It came out in the armoury hall. As she went down the sound of voices rose up to meet her—less subdued and funereal now as champagne was consumed, interspersed with laughter. She found herself listening out for Kit's voice amongst the others, and realised with a tearing sensation in her side that she'd never heard him laugh. Not really laugh, without irony or bitterness or cynicism.

But maybe he would be laughing now, with Olympia.

She came down the last step. The door was ahead of her, half-open and letting in arctic air and winter sunshine. Determined not to look round in case she lost her nerve, Sophie kept her head down and walked quickly towards it.

The cold air hit her as she stepped outside, making her gasp and bringing a rush of tears to her eyes. She sniffed hard, and brushed them impatiently away with the sleeve of her faithful old coat.

'So you're leaving.'

She whirled round. Kit was standing at the top of the steps, in the open doorway. His hands were in his pockets, his top button undone and his tie pulled loose, but despite all that there was still something sinister in his stillness, the rigid blankness of his face.

The last glowing embers of hope in Sophie's heart went out.

'Yes.' She nodded, and even managed a brief smile although meeting his eye was too much to attempt. 'I saw you talking to Olympia. It's a small world. I suppose she told you everything.'

'Yes. Not that it makes any difference. So now you're going—just like that. Were you going to say goodbye?'

Sophie kept her eyes fixed on the ivy growing up the wall by the steps, twining itself around an old cast-iron downpipe. Of course it didn't make any difference, she told herself numbly. He already knew she was nothing. Her voice seemed to come from very far away. 'I'll write to Tatiana. She's surrounded by friends at the moment—I don't want to barge in.'

'It was Jasper I was thinking of. What about him?'

Sophie moved her bag from one hand to the other. She was conscious of holding herself very upright, placing her feet carefully together, almost as if if she didn't take care to do this she might just collapse. She still couldn't bring herself to look at him.

'He'll be OK now. He doesn't need me.'

At the top of the steps Kit made some sudden movement. For a moment she thought he had turned and was going to go inside, but instead he dragged a hand through his hair and swung back to face her again. This time there was no disguising the blistering anger on his face.

'So, who is he? I mean, he's obviously pretty special that he's come all this way to claim you and you can't even wait until the funeral is over before you go and fall into bed with him. Is it the same one I heard you talking to on the train, or someone else?'

After a moment of confusion it dawned on Sophie that he must have seen her with Sergio. And jumped, instantly, to the wrong conclusion.

Except there wasn't really such a thing as a wrong conclusion. In her experience 'wrong conclusion' tended to mean the same thing as 'confirmation of existing prejudice', and she had learned long ago that no amount of logical explanations could alter people's prejudices. That had to come from within themselves.

'Someone else.'

'Do you love him?' Suddenly the anger that had gripped him seemed to vanish and he just sounded very tired. Defeated almost.

Sophie shook her head. Her knees were shaking, her chest burning with the effort of holding back the sobs that threatened to tear her apart.

'No.'

'Then why? Why are you going to him?'

'Because he'd fight for me.' She took a deep breath and lifted her head. In a voice that was completely calm, completely steady she said, 'Because he trusts me.'

And then she turned and began to walk away.

Blindly Kit shouldered his way through the people standing in the hall. Seeing his ashen face and the stricken expression on it, some of them exchanged loaded glances and murmured about grief striking even the strongest.

Reaching the library, he shut the door and leaned against it, breathing hard and fast.

Trust. That was the last thing he'd expected her to say.

He brought his hands up to his head, sliding his fingers into his hair as his mind raced. He had learned very early on in life that few people could be trusted, and since then he had almost prided himself on his cynicism. It meant he was one step ahead of the game and gave him immunity from the emotional disasters that felled others.

It also meant he had just had to watch the only woman he wanted to be with walk away from him, right into the arms of someone else. Someone who wore designer clothes and left his shirt tails trailing and *trusted* her. Someone who would fight for her.

Well, trust might not be his strong suit, but fighting was something he could do.

He threw open the door, and almost ran straight into the person who was standing right on the other side of it.

'Alexia, what the—?'

'I wanted to talk.' She recovered from her obvious fright pretty quickly, following him as he kept on walking towards the noise of the party. 'There's something I need to tell you.'

'Now isn't a good time,' he said, moving through the groups of people still standing in the portrait hall, gritting his teeth against the need to be far more brutally honest.

'I know. I'm sorry, but it's bothered me all these years.' She caught up with him as he went through the archway into the armoury hall and moved in front of him as he reached the door. 'That thing that happened at school. It wasn't Summer, it was Olympia. She set it all up. I mean, Summer—Sophie— did have the dress and I don't know how she got the money to pay for it, but it certainly wasn't by stealing it from the dorm. Olympia just said it was.'

'I know,' Kit said wearily. 'I never doubted that bit.'

'Oh.' Alexia had taken her hat off now, and without it she looked oddly exposed and slightly crestfallen. 'I know it's ages ago and it was just some silly schoolgirl prank, but hearing Olympia say it again like that, I didn't like it. We're adults now. I just wanted to make sure you knew the truth.'

'The truth is slightly irrelevant really. It's what we're prepared to believe that matters.' He hesitated, his throat suddenly feeling as if he'd swallowed arsenic. 'The other thing—about her checking into the hotel with a man. Was that one of Olympia's fabrications too?'

'No, that was true.' Alexia was looking at him almost imploringly. 'Kit—are you really OK? Can I help?'

From a great distance he recognised her pain as being similar to his own. It made him speak gently to her.

'No, I'm not. But you have already.'

He wove his way through the parked cars jamming the courtyard and broke into a run as he reached the tower gate. At the sides of the driveway the snow was still crisp and unmarked, but as he ran down he noticed the prints Sophie's high-heeled shoes had made and they made her feel closer—as if she hadn't really gone. When he reached the road through the village they were lost amongst everyone else's.

The King's Arms was in the mid-afternoon lull between lunchtime and evening drinkers. The landlord sat behind the bar reading the *Racing Times*, but he got to his feet as Kit appeared.

'Major Fitzroy. I mean Lord Fitzr—'

Kit cut straight through the etiquette confusion. 'I'm looking for someone,' he said harshly. 'Someone staying here. Room three I believe? I'll see myself up.'

Without giving the flustered landlord time to respond he headed for the stairs, taking them two at a time. Room three was at the end of the short corridor. An empty vodka bottle stood outside it. Kit hammered on the door.

'Sophie!'

Kit listened hard, but the only sounds were muted voices

from a television somewhere and the ragged rasp of his own breathing. His tortured mind conjured an image of the man he'd seen earlier pausing as he unzipped Sophie's dress and her whispering, *Don't worry—he'll go away...*

But he wouldn't. Not until he'd seen her.

'Sophie!'

Clenching his hand into a fist, he was just about to beat on the door again when it opened an inch. A face—puffy-eyed, swarthy, unshaven—peered out at him.

'She's not here.'

With a curse of pure rage, Kit put his shoulder to the door. Whoever it was on the other side didn't put up much resistance and the door opened easily. Glancing at him only long enough to register that he was naked except for a small white towel slung around his hips, Kit pushed past and strode into the room.

In a heartbeat he took in the clothes scattered over the floor—black clothes, like puddles of tar on the cream carpet—the wide bed with its passion-tumbled covers and the room darkened, and he thought he might black out.

'Kit—' Jasper leapt out of the bed, dragging the rumpled sheet and pulling it around himself. Blinking, Kit shook his head, trying to reconcile what he was actually seeing with what he had expected.

'Jasper?'

'Look, I didn't want you to find out like this.' Jasper paused and ducked his head for a moment, but then gathered himself and raised his head again, looking Kit squarely in the eye while the man in the white towel went to his side. 'But it's probably time you knew anyway. I can't go on hiding who I really am just because it doesn't fit the Fitzroy mould. I love Sergio. And I know what you're going to say but—'

Kit gave a short, incredulous laugh as relief burst through him. 'It's the best news I've had for a long time. Really. I can't tell you how pleased I am.' He turned and shook hands with the bewildered man in the white towel, and then went over to Jasper and embraced him briefly, hard. 'Now please—if Sophie's not here, where the hell is she?'

The smile faded from Jasper's face. 'She's gone. She's getting the train back to London. Kit, did something happen between you, because—?'

Kit turned away, putting his hands to his head as despair sucked him down. He swore savagely. Twice. And then strode to the door.

'Yes, something happened between us,' he said, turning back to Jasper with a suicidal smile. 'I was just too stupid to understand exactly what it was.'

The good news was that Sophie didn't have to wait long for a train to come. The bad news was that there was only one straight-through express service to London every day, and that was long gone. The one she boarded was a small, clanking local train that stopped at every miniature village station all along the line and terminated at Newcastle.

The train was warm and virtually empty. Sophie slunk to a seat in the corner and sat with her eyes closed so she didn't have to look at Alnburgh, transformed by the sinking sun into a golden fairy tale castle from an old-fashioned storybook, get swallowed up by the blue haze.

She was used to this, she told herself over and over. Moving on was what she did best. Hadn't she always felt panicked by the thought of permanence? She was good at new starts. Reinventing herself.

But until now she hadn't really known who 'herself' was. Sophie Greenham was a construction; a sort of patchwork of bits borrowed from films and books and other people, fragments of fact layered up with wistful half-truths and shameless lies, all carried off with enough chutzpah to make them seem credible.

Beneath Kit's cool, incisive gaze all the joins had dissolved and the pieces had fallen away. She was left just being herself. A person she didn't really know, who felt things she didn't usually feel and needed things she didn't understand.

As she got further away from Alnburgh her phone came back into signal range and texts began to come in with teeth-grating regularity. Biting her cheeks against each sledgehammer blow of disappointment, Sophie couldn't stop herself checking every time to see if any were from Kit.

They weren't.

There were several from her agent. The vampire film people wanted to see her again. The outfit had impressed *them*, at least.

'Tickets from Alnburgh.'

She opened her eyes. The guard was making his way along the swaying carriage towards her. She sat up, fumbling in her broken bag for her purse as she blinked away the stinging in her eyes.

'A single to London, please.'

The guard punched numbers into his ticket machine with pudgy fingers. 'Change at Newcastle,' he said without looking at her. 'The London train goes from platform two. It's a bit of a distance so you'll need to hurry.'

'Thank you,' Sophie muttered, trying to fix those details in her head. Until then she'd only thought as far as getting on this train. Arriving at Newcastle, getting off and taking herself forwards from there felt like stepping into a void.

She dug her nails into her palms and looked unseeingly out of the window as a wave of panic washed over her. Out of nowhere a thought occurred to her.

'Actually—can you make that two tickets?'

'Are you with someone?'

For the first time the guard looked at her properly; a glare delivered over the top of his glasses that suggested she was doing something underhand. The reality was she was just trying to put something right.

'No.' Sophie heard the break in her voice. 'No, I'm alone. But let's just say I had a debt to pay.'

The station at Alnburgh was, unsurprisingly, empty. Kit stood for a moment on the bleak platform, breathing hard from running and looking desperately around, as if in some part of his mind he still thought there was a chance she would be there.

She wasn't. Of course she wasn't. She had left, with infinite dignity, and for good.

He tipped his head back and breathed in, feeling the throb of blood in his temples, waiting until the urge to punch something had passed.

'Missed your train?'

Kit looked round. A man wearing overalls and a yellow high-vis jacket had appeared, carrying a spade.

'Something like that. When's the next one to London?'

The man went over to the grit bin at the end of the platform and thrust the spade into it.

'London? The only straight-through London train from here is the 11.07 in the morning. If you need to get one before that you'll have to get to Newcastle.' He threw the spadeful of grit across the compacted snow.

Hopelessness engulfed Kit. Numbly he started walking away. If he caught a train from Newcastle, by the time he'd got to London she'd be long gone and he'd have no way of finding her. Unless...

Unless...

He spun round. 'Wait a minute. Did you say the only straight-through train was this morning? So the one that just left...'

'Was the local service to Newcastle. That's right.'

'Thanks.'

Kit broke into a run. He didn't stop until he reached the tower gate, and remembered the cars. The party was evidently still going on, and the courtyard was still rammed with vehicles. Kit stopped. Bracing his arms against the shiny black bonnet of the one nearest to him, letting his head drop as ragged breaths were torn from his heaving chest, almost like sobs.

She had gone. And he couldn't even go after her.

'Sir?'

Dimly he was aware of the car door opening and a figure getting out. Until that point he hadn't registered which car he was leaning against, or that there was anyone in it, but now he saw that it was the funeral car and the grey-haired man who had just got out was the undertaker.

'I was going to ask if you were all right, but clearly that would be a daft question,' he said, abandoning the stiff formality of his role. 'A better question would be, is there anything I can do to help?'

'Yes,' Kit rasped. 'Yes, there is.'

Sophie stood on the platform and looked around in confusion.

Newcastle Central Station was a magnificent example of Victorian design and engineering. With its iron-boned canopy arching above her, Sophie felt as if she were standing in the belly of a vast whale.

Apart from the noise, and the crowds, maybe. Being inside a whale would probably be a blissfully quiet experience compared to this. People pushed past her, shouting into mobile phones to make themselves heard above the echoing announcement system and the noise of diesel engines.

Amongst them, Sophie felt tiny. Invisible.

It had been just a week and a half since she'd dashed onto

the 16.22 from King's Cross but now the girl with the stiletto boots and a corset dress and the who-cares attitude could barely bring herself to walk away from the little train that had brought her from Alnburgh. After the space and silence of the last ten days it felt as if the crowds were pressing in on her and that she might simply be swept away, or trampled underfoot. And that no one would notice.

But the guard had said she needed to hurry if she was going to catch the London connection. Adjusting her grip on her broken bag, holding it awkwardly to make sure it didn't spill its contents, she forced herself to move forwards.

Platform two. Where was platform two? Her eyes scanned the bewildering array of signs, but somehow none of the words made sense to her. Except one, high up on the lit-up board of train departures.

Alnburgh.

Sophie had never been homesick in her life, probably because she'd never really had a home to be sick for, but she thought the feeling might be something like the anguish that hollowed out her insides and filled her lungs with cement as she stared at the word.

She looked away. She didn't belong there—hadn't she told herself that countless times during the last ten days? The girl from nowhere with the made-up name and the made-up past didn't belong in a castle, or in a family with a thousand years of history.

So where did she belong?

Panic was rising inside her. Standing in the middle of the swarming station concourse, she suddenly felt as if she were falling, or disappearing, and there was nothing there to anchor her. She turned round, desperately searching for something familiar...

And then she saw him.

Pushing his way through the crowds of commuters, head

and shoulders above everyone else, his face tense and ashen but so beautiful that for a moment Sophie couldn't breathe. She stood, not wanting to take her eyes off him in case he disappeared again, unable to speak.

'Kit.'

It was a whisper. A whimper. So quiet she barely heard it herself. But at that moment he turned his head and looked straight at her.

His footsteps slowed, and for a second the expression on his face was one she hadn't seen before. Uncertainty. Fear. The same things she was feeling—or had been until she saw him. And then it was gone—replaced by a sort of scowling ferocity as he crossed the distance between them with long, rapid strides. Gathering her into his arms, he kissed her, hungrily and hard.

There were tears running down Sophie's face when she finally pulled away. She felt tender and torn with emotions she couldn't begin to unravel—gratitude and joy and relief, undercut with the terrible anguish she was beginning to realise went with loving someone.

'My train...' she croaked, steeling herself for the possibility that he'd just come to say goodbye.

Slowly he shook his head. His eyes didn't leave hers. 'Don't get on it.'

'Why not?'

He took her face between his hands, drawing her close to him so that in the middle of the crowd they were in their own private universe. Under his silver gaze Sophie felt as if she were bathed in moonlight.

'Because then I would have to get on it too,' he murmured gravely, 'and I'd have to sit opposite you for the next two and a half hours, looking at you, breathing in your scent and wanting to take your clothes off and make love to you on the table.' He gave her a rueful smile that made her heart turn over. 'I've done that once before, so I know how hard it is. And because I hijacked a hearse and committed several civil and traffic offences to find you, and now I have I don't want to let you go again. Not until I've said what I have to say. Starting with sorry.'

Tears were still spilling down her cheeks. 'Kit, you don't have to—'

'I've been rehearsing this all the way from Alnburgh,' he said, brushing the tears away with his thumbs, 'so if you could listen without interrupting that would be good. I saw Jasper.'

'Oh! And—'

He frowned. 'I'm horrified...'

Sophie's mouth opened in protest, but before she could say anything he kissed her into silence and continued softly, '...that he ever thought I wouldn't *approve*. Lord, am I such a judgmental bastard?'

Sophie gave a hiccupping laugh that was half sob. 'I think you're asking the wrong person.'

He let her go then, dropping his hands to his sides and looking down at her with an expression of abject desolation. 'God, Sophie, I'm so sorry. I've spent my whole miserable life not trusting anyone so it had become something of a habit. Until Olympia told me what she did to you at school and I wanted to wring her neck, and it made me realise that I trusted you absolutely.'

'But what about with Sergio—you thought—'

Out of his arms, without his touch Sophie felt as if she were breaking up again. The crowed swelled and jostled around them. A commuter banged her leg with his briefcase.

'No.' It was a groan of surrender. An admission of defeat. He pulled her back into his arms and held her against him so that she could feel the beat of his heart. 'I was too bloody deranged with jealousy to think at all. I just wanted to tear him limb from limb. I know it's not big or clever, but I can't help it. I just want you for myself.'

Tentatively she lifted her head to look up at him, her vision blurred by wonder and tears.

'Really?'

In reply he kissed her again, this time so tenderly that she felt as if he were caressing her soul.

'It'll never work,' she murmured against his mouth. 'I'm not good enough for you.'

'I think…' he kissed the corner of her mouth, her jaw '…we've already established that you're far too good for me.'

She closed her eyes as rapture spiralled through her. 'Socially I mean. I'm nobody.'

His lips brushed her ear lobe. 'So am I, remember?'

It was getting harder to concentrate. Harder to think of reasons why she shouldn't just give in to the rising tide of longing inside her. Harder to keep her knees from buckling. 'I'd be disastrous for your career,' she breathed. 'Amongst all those officers' wives—'

He lifted his head and gazed at her with eyes that were lit by some inner light. 'You'll outshine them all,' he said softly, simply. 'They'll want to hate you for being so beautiful but they won't be able to. Now, have you any more objections?'

'No.'

He seized her hand. 'Then for God's sake let's go and find the nearest hotel.'

Still Sophie held back. 'But I thought you had to report back for duty…'

'I called in some favours.' Gently he took her face between his hands and kissed her again. 'I have three weeks' compassionate leave following my father's death. But since Ralph wasn't actually my father I think we can just call it passionate leave. I intend to make the most of every second.'

EPILOGUE

IT WAS just a tiny piece in the property section of one of the Sunday papers. Eating brioche spread thickly with raspberry jam in the crumpled ruins of the bed that had become their world for the last three weeks, Sophie gave a little squeal.

'Listen to this!

'Unexpected Twist to Fitzroy Inheritance.
'Following the recent death of Ralph Fitzroy, eighth Earl of Hawksworth and owner of the Alnburgh estate, it has come to light that the expected heir is not, in fact, set to inherit. Sources close to the family have confirmed that the estate, which includes Alnburgh Castle and five hundred acres of land in Northumberland as well as a sizeable slice of premium real estate in Chelsea, will pass to Jasper Fitzroy, the Earl's younger son from his second marriage, rather than his older brother, Major Kit Fitzroy.'

Putting the last bit of brioche in her mouth, she continued,

'Major Fitzroy, a serving member of the armed forces, was recently awarded the George Medal for bravery. However, it's possible that his courage failed him when it came to taking on Alnburgh. According to locals, maintenance of the estate has been severely neglected in recent years, leaving the next owner with a heavy financial burden to bear. While Kit Fitzroy is rumoured to have considerable personal wealth, perhaps this is one rescue mission he just doesn't want to take on...'

She tossed the newspaper aside and, licking jam off her fingers, cast Kit a sideways glance from under her lashes.

'"Considerable personal wealth"?' She wriggled down beneath the covers, smiling as she kissed his shoulder. 'I like the sound of that.'

Kit, still surfacing from the depths of the sleep he'd been blessed with since he'd had Sophie in his bed, arched an eyebrow.

'I thought as much,' he sighed, turning over and looking straight into her sparkling, beautiful eyes. 'You're nothing but a shallow, cynical gold-digger.'

'You're right.' Sophie nodded seriously, pressing her lips together to stop herself from smiling. 'To be honest, I'm really only interested in your money, and your exceptionally gorgeous Chelsea house.' The sweeping gesture she made with her arm took in the bedroom with its view of the garden square outside. 'It's why I've decided to put up with your boring personality and frankly quite average looks. Not to mention your disappointing performance in bed—'

She broke off with a squeal as, beneath the sheets, he slid a languid hand between her thighs.

'Sorry, what was that?' he murmured gravely.

'I said...' she gasped '...that I was only interested in your... money.' He watched her eyes darken as he moved his hand higher. 'I've always wanted to be a rich man's plaything.'

He propped himself up on one elbow, so he could see her better. Her hair was spilling over the pillow—a gentler red than when he'd first seen her that day on the train—the colour of horse chestnuts rather than holly berries—and her face was bare of make-up. She had never looked more beautiful.

'Not a rich man's wife?' he asked idly, leaning down to kiss the hollow above her collarbone.

'Oh, no. If we're talking marriage I'd be looking for a title as well as a fortune.' Her voice turned husky as his lips moved to the base of her throat. 'And a sizeable estate to go with it...'

He smiled, taking his time, breathing in the scent of her skin. 'OK, that's good to know. Since I'm fresh out of titles and estates there's probably no point in asking.'

He felt her stiffen, heard her little gasp of shock and excitement. 'Well, there might be some room for negotiation,' she said breathlessly. 'And I'd say that right now you're in a pretty good bargaining position...'

'Sophie Greenham,' he said gravely, 'I love you because you are beautiful and clever and honest and loyal...'

'Flattery will get you a very long way,' she sighed, closing her eyes as his fingertips trailed rapture over the quivering skin on the inside of her thighs. 'And *that* will probably do the rest...'

His chest tightened as he looked down at her. 'I love you because you think underwear is a better investment than clothes, and because you're brave and funny and sexy, and I was wondering if you'd possibly consider marrying me?'

Her eyes opened and met his. The smile that spread slowly across her face was one of pure, incredulous happiness. It felt like watching the sun rise.

'Yes,' she whispered, gazing up at him with dazed, brilliant eyes. 'Yes, please.'

'I feel it's only fair to warn you that I've been disowned by my family...'

Serene, she took his face in her hands. 'We can make our own family.'

He frowned, smoothing a strand of hair from her cheek, suddenly finding it difficult to speak for the lump of emotion in his throat. 'And I have no title, no castle and no lands to offer you.'

She laughed, pulling him down into her arms. 'Believe me, I absolutely wouldn't have it any other way...'

* * * * *

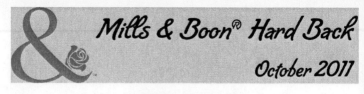

Mills & Boon® Hard Back
October 2011

ROMANCE

The Most Coveted Prize	Penny Jordan
The Costarella Conquest	Emma Darcy
The Night that Changed Everything	Anne McAllister
Craving the Forbidden	India Grey
The Lost Wife	Maggie Cox
Heiress Behind the Headlines	Caitlin Crews
Weight of the Crown	Christina Hollis
Innocent in the Ivory Tower	Lucy Ellis
Flirting With Intent	Kelly Hunter
A Moment on the Lips	Kate Hardy
Her Italian Soldier	Rebecca Winters
The Lonesome Rancher	Patricia Thayer
Nikki and the Lone Wolf	Marion Lennox
Mardie and the City Surgeon	Marion Lennox
Bridesmaid Says, 'I Do!'	Barbara Hannay
The Princess Test	Shirley Jump
Breaking Her No-Dates Rule	Emily Forbes
Waking Up With Dr Off-Limits	Amy Andrews

HISTORICAL

The Lady Forfeits	Carole Mortimer
Valiant Soldier, Beautiful Enemy	Diane Gaston
Winning the War Hero's Heart	Mary Nichols
Hostage Bride	Anne Herries

MEDICAL ROMANCE™

Tempted by Dr Daisy	Caroline Anderson
The Fiancée He Can't Forget	Caroline Anderson
A Cotswold Christmas Bride	Joanna Neil
All She Wants For Christmas	Annie Claydon

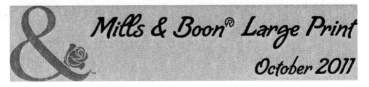

Mills & Boon® Large Print

October 2011

ROMANCE

Passion and the Prince	Penny Jordan
For Duty's Sake	Lucy Monroe
Alessandro's Prize	Helen Bianchin
Mr and Mischief	Kate Hewitt
Her Desert Prince	Rebecca Winters
The Boss's Surprise Son	Teresa Carpenter
Ordinary Girl in a Tiara	Jessica Hart
Tempted by Trouble	Liz Fielding

HISTORICAL

Secret Life of a Scandalous Debutante	Bronwyn Scott
One Illicit Night	Sophia James
The Governess and the Sheikh	Marguerite Kaye
Pirate's Daughter, Rebel Wife	June Francis

MEDICAL ROMANCE™

Taming Dr Tempest	Meredith Webber
The Doctor and the Debutante	Anne Fraser
The Honourable Maverick	Alison Roberts
The Unsung Hero	Alison Roberts
St Piran's: The Fireman and Nurse Loveday	Kate Hardy
From Brooding Boss to Adoring Dad	Dianne Drake

ROMANCE

The Power of Vasilii	Penny Jordan
The Real Rio D'Aquila	Sandra Marton
A Shameful Consequence	Carol Marinelli
A Dangerous Infatuation	Chantelle Shaw
Kholodov's Last Mistress	Kate Hewitt
His Christmas Acquisition	Cathy Williams
The Argentine's Price	Maisey Yates
Captive but Forbidden	Lynn Raye Harris
On the First Night of Christmas...	Heidi Rice
The Power and the Glory	Kimberly Lang
How a Cowboy Stole Her Heart	Donna Alward
Tall, Dark, Texas Ranger	Patricia Thayer
The Secretary's Secret	Michelle Douglas
Rodeo Daddy	Soraya Lane
The Boy is Back in Town	Nina Harrington
Confessions of a Girl-Next-Door	Jackie Braun
Mistletoe, Midwife...Miracle Baby	Anne Fraser
Dynamite Doc or Christmas Dad?	Marion Lennox

HISTORICAL

The Lady Confesses	Carole Mortimer
The Dangerous Lord Darrington	Sarah Mallory
The Unconventional Maiden	June Francis
Her Battle-Scarred Knight	Meriel Fuller

MEDICAL ROMANCE™

The Child Who Rescued Christmas	Jessica Matthews
Firefighter With A Frozen Heart	Dianne Drake
How to Save a Marriage in a Million	Leonie Knight
Swallowbrook's Winter Bride	Abigail Gordon

Mills & Boon® Large Print
November 2011

ROMANCE

The Marriage Betrayal	Lynne Graham
The Ice Prince	Sandra Marton
Doukakis's Apprentice	Sarah Morgan
Surrender to the Past	Carole Mortimer
Her Outback Commander	Margaret Way
A Kiss to Seal the Deal	Nikki Logan
Baby on the Ranch	Susan Meier
Girl in a Vintage Dress	Nicola Marsh

HISTORICAL

Lady Drusilla's Road to Ruin	Christine Merrill
Glory and the Rake	Deborah Simmons
To Marry a Matchmaker	Michelle Styles
The Mercenary's Bride	Terri Brisbin

MEDICAL ROMANCE™

Her Little Secret	Carol Marinelli
The Doctor's Damsel in Distress	Janice Lynn
The Taming of Dr Alex Draycott	Joanna Neil
The Man Behind the Badge	Sharon Archer
St Piran's: Tiny Miracle Twins	Maggie Kingsley
Maverick in the ER	Jessica Matthews